CW01433052

THE PAGES OF THE SEA

THE
PAGES
OF
THE
SEA

Anne Hawk

WEATHERGLASS BOOKS

For Shraddhajit

THE
PAGES
OF
THE
SEA

1

Thursday evening it was just Wheeler and Celeste on the property, out near the concrete sink built against the house. Wheeler sat on the retaining wall that anchored the two-storey building to the slope. Celeste stood to the rear of her, on the concrete landing, having appeared from the entrance to the house.

Wheeler watched as her aunt strayed back in through the side entrance.

Tant'Celeste di' come out an go back in a few times now.

Wheeler's forehead puckered as she tried to work out what her aunt was doing; her smooth, black skin unstitched, and she went back to staring at the other side of the bay.

A clock tower stood at the height of the long headland opposite. A strand of gemstone clouds hung to the left, out beyond the harbour. With the descent of the sun, darkness lurked here and there in the hills surrounding the bay.

Built on a slope, the five-bedroomed house was bounded by sharp volcanic rock on one side and a dry terraced garden on its other side. The steep volcanic yard was a relic of the centuries-old eruption that had fashioned the bay crater and the arena of hills. The faded walls of the family house bristled in the hard yellow light of the evening sun. Wheeler had come to live in the house two months earlier, after her mother left the island to work overseas in England. She and her two teenage sisters now lived with their aunts and three cousins. Each month a postal order arrived from England covering the sisters' room and board.

"Y'could tell me whey dem chil'ren gone, huh? Ah carnt self see *one* o dem t'run a errand?"

Wheeler once again stared at Celeste.

She ant di' ask questions in nobody suppose t'answer.

Wheeler didn't answer this one.

Celeste cocked her head. "Adele! Hesta… Jon-a-ton!" she shouted. "Y'could tell me whey dat bwoy gone?"

Wheeler stared with her. No one appeared from behind the house or from the bushes to the side of the yard.

"Go round the back o' d'house, see if Adele an dem in up dere."

Wheeler sprang to her feet. "Yes, Tant'Celeste." She scaled the rocky yard in search of Adele and Hesta, and her cousin Jonathan.

"Jon-a-ton! A-dele! *Hesta*!" Wheeler wailed, coming upright at the top of the yard. There was no one to the right of the washing line; no one on the darkening path at the back of the house. She scrambled to the other side of the house. No one in the terraced yard, with its dry garden of shrubs and vines. She made her way towards the Cut, an open-air stairway on the edge of the place. Lined on both sides by low trees and arid dry-season bush, the shallow concrete steps shot up to an overhead lane.

Wheeler stared uphill at the narrow steps.

No sign o' she sisters.

The Cut continued downhill. There was a straight run of steps between where she stood and a lower entrance to the house. Much further down, the steps took a sudden turn to the left against a string of small wooden houses. Narrowing her eyes, Wheeler peered.

Jonaton in knocking about wid dem bwoys down dere.

She thumped her way down the rocky side of the house and reported back.

"Adele and Hesta in up dere. Dey mus still be in Guides." She waited. "Y'warnt ah go in d'Guide Hall, Tant'Celeste, an say y'warnt dem t'come home? Ah in know whey Jonaton gone," she added.

A small vein jumped in Celeste's neck. There was a crowd of little plaits on her head. She turned and went back into the house.

A thin line appeared on Wheeler's face.

She di' still getting used t'she ant. She dint know how she goan act sometimes.

Her small chest still heaving, Wheeler caught her breath. She studied the empty air where Celeste had stood.

3

The deep waters of St Catherine's Bay darkened against the line of the shore. The tide never ebbed, day or night. The Caribbean Sea never rolled out.

The formation of little clouds was now unravelling.

"Y'tink y'can go on d'Wharf? See wha dey hav left in d'shop? Dere in a singul slice o' bread in d'house."

Celeste had returned. Wheeler twisted round.

Bread rolls and loaves for the large household were baked on Saturday afternoons. Later in the week, once the bread was all gone, one of the older children would be sent to the shop to buy more.

"Y'tink y'can go on d'Wharf?"

Wheeler saw herself reflected in Celeste's tired eyes – the small bouquet of school ribbons still on her head. She watched her aunt bend down to her level: red dollar bill in her hand, paper sack in the other, a shadowy question on her face.

"Y'tink y'can go down an get d'bread… An ain let nobody see you?"

Go on Wharf Road by sheself?

Wheeler took a look at the clock tower, took a hard look at herself standing beside it in her aunt's eyes. Some questions needed answering. "Y-es, Tant'Celeste," she said.

St Catherine's Bay was a seafront of effortless beauty. A sweeping horseshoe inlet rising up from the sea, its shelf-like terraces and hills negotiated by steps: steps leading to red-roofed buildings or descending from overhead roads; steps made of concrete, cobble or wood cut into the circling slopes. So that residents were all the while either crawling up or else thundering down steps.

Arriving at the Cut, Wheeler glanced up at the long arrow of overhead steps. The woof of night herons in her ears, she launched over the jumble of steps pointing downhill. She filed her way between a set of older boys standing liming where the Cut turned. "Whey Donelle?" one of them said.

"He gone f'heself," she answered.

Donelle was Wheeler's youngest cousin. Following their latest row, he'd taken off to play by himself. The same age, they spent their time in each other's company more often than not.

"Whey Jon-a-ton?" another boy asked. Wheeler didn't bother answering that.

E'rybody know Jonaton don't knock about wid her an Donelle.

There were children younger than her playing at a standpipe. Wheeler rushed past them, taking the final forty steps to the bottom road.

Go past d'cinema – hear me do – to d'corner. Take yer time, do. Don't run…

On Russell Street, she flew across the road. The white and blue walls of the Phoenix Cinema reared up to her left from its location on Wharf Road. The most prominent building on the waterfront, the cinema was surrounded by red gravel. A flight of steps led into the gravel yard.

The rest of Celeste's words played on in Wheeler's mind.

Go past d'cinema gate. Cross d'gap by d'rum shop.

Wheeler pressed her face against the rusted metal gate and stared at the grey cinema steps. The gate was always locked except on Saturdays and when there was a filmshow on. A handful of kids were climbing over the bottom gate by the shore. One of them leapt down and yelled back at the others from the red gravel yard.

Big kids does do wha dey warnt.

Wheeler drifted away. She took the long way to the bread shop, going along Russell Street.

The evening before, she and Donelle had heard the steel band from above, on the lane. She heard it tuning up now in the band pit on Wharf Road. In a few weeks' time it would be carnival. Warm tinkerings of sound echoed along the soft asphalt, reverberated through her thin flip-flops.

Coming clear of a row of houses, Wheeler glanced up. She'd arrived at the gap between Russell Street and the shore, an acreage of sand with low, tough grass. She looked towards the steelband pit in the distance, its galvanised roof dwarfed by the massive cinema wall. The warm-up continued: abrupt broken-off melodies, individual twists and turns.

To the right, on the opposite side of the gap, a yellow light bulb signalled the bread shop's location. A slick rush of gold, the orange sea swirled at the edge of Wharf Road.

Wheeler's features stiffened. Balancing on the edge of Russell Street, she leaned towards the grassy underside of the road.

Ain let nobody see you.

She took off down the rocky bank.

2

The house Wheeler now lived in had been her mother's childhood home. Situated on a narrow wedge of land part way up the slope, surrounded by bush and rocks, it was built over a number of years by Wheeler's grandparents. They had started out with a high galvanised roof rigged to an open-sided frame. The kitchen and a downstairs bedroom were filled in first, followed by a side veranda and three upstairs rooms, reached via the sloped terraced yard. More bedrooms were added as each of their four daughters was born. In time, the inside stairway was built. Ahead of the rainy season, rough-mixed cement was thrown down over most of the surrounding ground to stop it turning to mud.

Dry season. No threat of rain now.

Wheeler walked onto the upstairs landing dressed in her school uniform, a soft satchel slung across her chest. She slowed down. There were scrambling voices in the bedroom shared by Donelle and Jonathan; a louder, domineering voice in the end bedroom belonging to their older brother, Floyd.

There were eight people in total living in the house: the three brothers, Wheeler, her sisters and their two aunts. Peaceful the evening before, the house now rustled with the unseen presence of others and the growing sense of a row.

"All-you playing y'in hear!"

Wheeler inched her way along the landing, getting away from the trouble. She hurried down the stairs.

The kitchen was marred by grim shadows at this time of the day, the sun having yet to crest the treeline at the top of the hill. It was a room into which the sun shone only in late afternoon like an afterthought. On the counter was some of the bread Wheeler had bought the previous evening.

Celeste had asked: "Who see you?"

"Nobody, Tant'Celeste," Wheeler had answered, handing over the paper sack and change.

Now, as Wheeler went out into the yard, Celeste was at the large concrete sink shucking at a juking board, her gaunt collarbone joggling inside a dingy housedress. Wheeler gravitated towards Celeste like the tide towards a shuddering moon.

Tant'Celeste di' always busy – jus like dey mudda. Else she looking f'sumting t'do.

Celeste did not look up. If she had the sense of being scrutinised or compared to someone else, she betrayed no sign of it.

Tant'Celeste di' say *do* like old people, even self she in old.

Wheeler paused just far enough to stop water spitting off the juking board from wetting her blue and white uniform.

There was a line of clothes pegs down the front of Celeste's faded housedress. They might have been holding it together. The wooden pegs nodded as Celeste's hands pulled up and heaved down against the juking board. Wheeler's eyes lifted and then dipped with the clothes pegs as she waited beside Celeste. Below them, a small tug grunted over the long stretch of the bay on the way out to sea.

Celeste glanced up at the clock over on Church Street. "Whey yer sister?"

"She upstairs dolling up she hair."

"Urr-*hm*." A knowing look on her face, Celeste nodded. Lifting a bed sheet then wringing it, she dropped the sheet into a metal pail. The dim focus of her eyes landed on Wheeler. "Mind yerself – do," she said.

Wheeler stepped back. Her eyes followed Celeste up the yard.

Dey ant does say *do*… She di' hav a baby dat di' die a long time ago, Donelle did say. He in know when.

Celeste carried the pail up the incline, her hair the usual scramble of little plaits. *Wha d'point in dolling up y'hair?* her careless appearance seemed to say. *Wha d'point in anyting?* Straightening at the top of the yard, she lifted the white bed sheet out of the pail.

Adele, the eldest of Wheeler's sisters, clipped round the kitchen doorway, hair pulled up in a circle comb. "Le' we go," she said, cruising past Wheeler.

From the top of the yard, Celeste watched them hurrying. Adele descended to the front of the house. Face upturned, she shouted: "Tant'Celeste, we going."

Wheeler swirled around: "Tant'Celeste, we going."

As she approached the dense shadow cast by the house, Wheeler glanced back.

She tink she di'hear she ant say "Urr-*hm*".

Adele went hurtling downhill. They were running late again.

Was Adele fault dey running late!

Clutching the cloth satchel, Wheeler fastened her eyes on her sister's shirt collar, sliver of chevron tie underneath… kept her eyes glued to Adele, would not take her eyes off her, would tumble if she did. A glint of something as they took the turn: Adele's prefect badge.

"*A-dele*!"

Her sister stopped and looked round, schoolbooks pressed to her chest. "Y'in see we late? We hav fardah t'go now we in living in town."

Wasn't she fault dey running late.

"Why we in leave d'house fore now?"

"Why y'arguing?"

It was Adele's job to take Wheeler to school. It was Hesta's job to take her home.

11

Adele carried on downhill, a little slower than before.

Flotillas of schoolchildren bustled along Russell Street, white school shirts bobbing in the sun. Chalk-white walls, blue piping, the cinema building beamed in the early light, a giant wedding cake abandoned by the shore. At the gap, where the road turned, there was a squat pitch pine structure. The rum shop. One of its padlocked windows was cut higher than the other. From its narrow roadside lot, the rum shop appeared to be squinting at the view.

A few people were making their way across the gap to Wharf Road. The sea was no longer golden. The band pit stood empty. The bread shop had become anonymous on the edge of the opening without its heralding light.

"Watch whey y'going."

Wheeler trotted alongside Adele.

At the junction with Cable Street, lines of schoolchildren gave way to vehicles climbing up from the street below. Adele traded places with Wheeler, taking to the outside on the shoulderless road.

Wheeler looked to the unshaded view up ahead and screwed up her face.

D'walk did come longer – it di' come hotter since dey stop living in town.

Most days she was sweating by the time she arrived at school.

They had lived on Mallory Street, one of a trio of long,

slow roads hanging from the ridge above town. The entrance to Adele's school could be seen at the top of the road. The journey to school had taken fifteen minutes, compared to almost forty minutes now. Quarter to eight in the mornings, Wheeler and Adele would climb to the secondary school gate and carry on walking to the small five-dollar primer on Clarkton Road – the school intended to turn Wheeler into a scholarship girl. Both of her sisters had attended the primer before Wheeler. No luck with Hesta. The hope was Wheeler would succeed like Adele.

These days they left the house at quarter past seven. Or twenty past – even half past on occasion. Not having troubled her before, time seemed all the while to be shoving Wheeler around.

Stamping along in her whitewashed Keds, she kept up with Adele. Sweat beaded on Wheeler's shining forehead, gathered in the partings of her hair.

They approached the crooked junction where King Street, Columbus Street, Clarkton Road and Russell Street met. "Come, na!" Adele complained.

Wheeler's head shot round. Her small hand tugged at her sister's arm. "Adele! Somebody call yer name." A devil look came into Adele's eyes.

A wooden traffic box hung over the junction up ahead. In the box stood a gloved policewoman. She signalled for Adele, Wheeler and a procession of schoolchildren to come forward, having stopped the traffic in all directions.

The sisters left the others and veered off to the right, climbing to the street above. As they were about to go their separate ways on Clarkton Road, Adele reached out and placed a hand on Wheeler's shoulder. Now that they were alone, she delivered a lesson to her younger sister, talking right into her face.

"Jus because some street-liming fool wid no ambition – no sense – decide t'call *my* name out in d'street… don't mean *y'hav t'tell me.*"

"No, Adel—"

"Don't mean ah hav to pay dem *no* mind!"

"No, A-de—"

"How much time ah hav t'tell y'dat?"

She dint t-tell…

"H-uh? How much time?"

No response.

Adele stormed off. Her blue skirt and white shirt seemed to ignite as she turned.

Wheeler's thoughts became mixed up. She strived for words, but they would not come out. Grabbing hold of the strap on her satchel, Wheeler seethed.

But she dint tell her dat!

A line of cars stretched away from the traffic box. Sunlight pelted their chromework. Wheeler strolled on, eyes down, slowing at the opening to the hilltop primer.

Standing on a ledge two storeys high, the rectangular

14

building was a good distance away from the road. Between patches of brown grass, a dozen or more children in blue and white uniforms were climbing up a winding gravel path. Wheeler started following them. Some pupils were already making their way into the lower half of the yellow house. Others hung back on the flattened grass. As the path twisted, a new aspect of the bay appeared in the distance to Wheeler's left – a curved seam of water with a cluster of low grey buildings, a view of the docks not visible from the family house.

Who took d'cookie from d'cookie jar?

A knot of singing girls stood in the beaten-down grass. Wheeler stopped nearby, watching, wondering: *Who?*

One of the girls moved aside. Wheeler slipped her school bag to the ground and slotted into the gap. The quick-clapping circle of hands closed shut.

Who took d'cookie from d'cookie jar?

Who took d'cookie from d'cookie jar?

Number five took d'cookie from d'cookie jar!…

The game fell apart when a boy appeared on the lower stairway, ringing a bell. Wheeler ran towards it with the other children, then rushed back to retrieve her satchel.

Three large, open rooms faced a passage that ran along the width of the school – north to south. The teacher's desk was situated midway along, with a full view of the centre room and a partial view of the two end rooms. Walking past the teacher's desk to the right of the open doorway, Wheeler carried on to the next classroom, following another girl.

The room was painted a greyish green. There was a wide blackboard on the dividing wall between Wheeler's classroom and the centre room. Four rows of desks faced neat, precise writing on the board. The lengthy passages on the board were divided by a straight line drawn down the middle.

Seated on the nearside of the room, Wheeler gazed at the writing on her side of the board. There were gaps and sentences, sentences and still more gaps. The long, broken passage was part familiar, part not. The sentences on the far side of the board were for the older children in the room.

"All-you write dat down," said the teacher.

Wheeler glanced at the empty page in her exercise book. The clap-hand song started up in her head as the teacher tap-tapped the date at the top of the board.

"All y'know wha all-you doing," the teacher said, before leaving the room. "Every one o' dese words in d'gaps, all-you already know."

Doubtful, Wheeler focused on the board as the teacher repeated the same instructions in the two neighbouring rooms.

"All y'know wha all-you doing. Y'know every one o' dese words."

A whistling silence soon replaced the teacher's voice in the quiet school.

Wheeler frowned as she reread the passage on the board, gaps and all.

Gazing out at the teacher's desk, one of the longed-for words came into her head: *expectation*. After writing the date in the top right-hand corner, Wheeler started copying the passage into her book.

Lunchtime, Clarkton Road teemed with schoolchildren. Scholars from the house-school. A blitz of children from the elementary school threatened to spill onto the road. Crowds of them streamed up from the low forecourt. Still others stood liming at the top of the steps in their grey and blue and white uniforms.

The elementary school was where Hesta and Wheeler's cousins went to school. Wheeler waited at the side of Clarkton Road for Hesta to take her home.

No sign yet of Hesta.

Wheeler's body tensed in anticipation. She pressed the school bag to her side.

Some of the house-school scholars had wandered towards the police junction where the road grew wide. A red estate car pulled up and three of them climbed in. As the estate drove past, Wheeler pulled back. She tipped forward on spotting her sister.

Dressed in white shirt and navy skirt, tall, Hesta stood

near the centre of the wide school steps. Her shoulders sailed above the heads of the other teenagers. Not looking at Wheeler, she started talking to another girl.

Cars, trucks and swaying kids competed in the glittering midday sun.

Wheeler's eyes remained fixed on Hesta. It was Hesta's responsibility to guide her younger sister across the busy road.

As if remembering something, Hesta broke off talking to the other girl. She glanced sideways at Wheeler and shouted, "Run!"

Wheeler leapt at the road and ran.

3

Thin afternoon cloud held steady across the windless sky. The sun now stood over the entrance to the bay, with the gnaw of salt water in the air. Wheeler and Donelle turned onto the lane at the top of the Cut. It was still too early for the full band practice, but the intermittent peal of a solitary steelpan rang in the air above their heads. Warm orange light hugged the sides of their necks as they drifted up the crumbling narrow road.

Donelle wore a part-buttoned shirt with loose khaki shortpants. Retrieving a pebble from his pocket, he threw it at the rocky slope to their right: *Crack!* Stone on stone. Not turning round, Wheeler strode on up the spur, wearing an undervest and pinafore dress.

The cousins were the same age and the same height. They had known each other from Sunday school, but had become close friends since Wheeler had come to live in the family house. They attended different schools and spent the rest of their time wandering about and falling out. Having quarrelled the evening before, they'd made up now.

A young woman sat outside a weatherboard house on the underside of the road. "All-you awright?" she asked them.

"Yeh…"

"Aw-w-right," Donelle answered.

Wheeler started walking backwards, balancing on the edge of the road. Donelle copied her. He'd been telling her about what happened that morning as he got ready for school. "He coulnt find he pan sticks. Floyd make me and Jonaton look f'dem. Fore we leave d'house."

"Why he hit all-you?"

Donelle shrugged and lowered his head. "Jonaton say, 'Le' him find he own damn pan sticks.'" Stepping off the wall, he defended Jonathan: "He dint say it loud. Floyd come in, an he giv d'two o' us two hard *rap*. Say he goan giv us a licking if we in find he pan sticks fore we go t'school."

Wheeler stepped down off the ledge, lips pursed. She thought about the morning journey to school with Adele. Her sisters were always styling her off. But she knew this was worse.

They inhabited nights of dim light or no light at all. Swathes of the island remained untouched by electricity, served only by candlelight or by hurricane lamps, including some of the houses nearby.

Inside the family house, the dark stairway tumbled down

from the landing, took a sudden swerve in the middle and then continued headlong to the cracked kitchen floor. Wheeler sat near the top of the stairs, Donelle at the middle landing. They waited for their supper. A naked light bulb hung towards the centre of the room, casting its half-hearted light into the well of the kitchen. The cruel scent of kerosene, the smell of the sun-dried cacao crept its way up to Wheeler, making her stomach curl. Cheap and filling, cocoa tea was drunk mornings and at night.

Adele and Celeste worked alongside one another in the kitchen, Celeste turning the contents of a basin, Adele laying out enamel plates while casting an eye on the tall cocoa pot on the stove.

"Catch!" Donelle tossed a small beanbag up to Wheeler, his aim haphazard.

Lunging for the beanbag, Wheeler grazed her elbow against the rough edge of the stairs. She flung the beanbag back at him.

An older boy squeezed past Wheeler and came down the stairs. "We going f'a walk?" Donelle asked him.

Jonathan glanced at both of them and shrugged. "Ah in know," he said.

There was a clear resemblance between Jonathan and Donelle. Though the high forehead, pinched and ruffled on Donelle, shone with a light of optimism on Jonathan's face. Two years older than Wheeler and Donelle, he didn't spend much time with them, tending to lime with older

21

boys. He spent his free time playing marbles and cricket – an old piece of board for a bat. And staying away from Floyd.

Jonathan sat further down.

"Awright, we ready!" yelled Celeste.

All three went down the stairs.

Wheeler balanced a white enamel cup and plate as she made her way back up, followed by Donelle. There was a small serving of saltfish souse, half a boiled egg, plus a small slice of bread on both their plates. She placed the hot cup on the step above, sat down and started eating. Wheeler watched Jonathan take his food outside, followed by Adele carrying two supper plates.

Last to settle, Celeste sat on a chair facing the black doorway. There were still two large plates left unclaimed on the kitchen counter and two big cups. The L-shaped counter started at the bottom of the stairs and ran under the wide front windows, ending at a metal sink. A collection of lime and orange peel hung drying above the kitchen sink. A kerosene stove stood next to it, ticking.

"Wha y'waiting for?"

Wheeler pulled in. Floyd was coming down the stairs.

Floyd paused and hovered between Wheeler and Donelle. His arms and neck were thick, powerful-looking. Donelle shoved his meal to the side. He curled upright off the middle step and headed down.

Wheeler's eyes travelled up to Floyd's flat, broad face.

Her expression hardened. She remembered what Donelle said had happened over Floyd's missing steelpan sticks.

Donelle now came back up from the belly of the kitchen, carrying one of the unclaimed cups and supper plates. As their paths crossed, Floyd glared at him. Wheeler watched Donelle take the cup and plate up to his mother's bedroom.

She only hav t'go up dere when she in trouble.

Floyd's eyes landed on Wheeler. A hint of curiosity – of surprise – as he looked at her. He seemed to be mulling something over. Having collected his cup and plate, he sat at the counter near the foot of the stairs. His eyes now focused on the back of Celeste's head – a cold, harsh stare.

Later, in the small bedroom she shared with her sisters, Wheeler complained about Floyd's treatment of Donelle and Jonathan.

"He pan stick dere whey he leave dem. On d'veranda. Still he hitting dem."

"Mind y'biznis," Hesta snapped, not looking up.

Why she hav t'mind she biznis?

Wheeler lowered her head, shrinking into herself.

Hesta was leaning against the windowsill, her blunt face turned sideways, her long body stretched over a textbook. She held a hovering pencil in one hand, using the window ledge as a desk. Younger, taller than Adele, Hesta's manner was not as smooth as Adele's.

From the corner of her eye, Wheeler peered. Her gaze

lingered on Adele. "Why ah carnt say nutting? Ah jus tinking bout Donelle an dem—"

Adele glanced up, shook her head. "Don't say nutting bout Floyd."

She and Wheeler were sitting on the bed doing their homework under the frail overhead light, Wheeler doing sums on her working-out slate, Adele at the foot of the bed, busy writing.

The large brass bed had belonged to their mother and father. The bedroom had been Donelle's before he'd been moved next door. There was a shoulder-high cupboard near the head of the bed crammed with ironed school clothes and church clothes. A large cardboard box full of jumbled homeclothes sat opposite the bed on the floor. Their books and shoes and other belongings were piled either side of it. The little bedroom was full of the sisters, their schoolbooks and everything they owned.

Eyes returning to her slate, Wheeler continued adding up.

When it come t'styling people off, Hesta d'worse 'n Adele. She did come worse since dey mudda leave.

Wheeler cut her eye on Hesta. "When we mudda sending f'us?" she asked, glancing up.

"Wha's the answer f'dat?" asked Hesta, leaning towards Adele.

Adele took away the heavy textbook. She handed it back, having scribbled in it with a stubby pencil. Hesta often needed help.

Wheeler tried again: "Why we mudda hav t'go—"

"Y'awready know why," said Hesta.

"Times hard. She coulnt find enough money t'mind us," Adele explained.

"Wha if we farda come f'us? Wha if he looking f'us—"

"Sch-ups." Hesta kissed her teeth. "Why y'in go t'sleep?"

Wheeler kept her eyes on Adele.

Dey mudda di' leave fore Christmas. She dint know when dey farda leave.

"He might be looking f'us."

Putting down her pen, Adele fixed her eyes on Wheeler and shook her head. No, he wasn't looking for them.

Their father had left the island before Wheeler was old enough to talk. In fallow times he would go looking for work in Aruba. The final time he'd stopped writing, had stopped sending money home.

"Go t'*sleep*!"

Wheeler rolled onto her back. She slipped her slate under the bed and gazed off to the side window. Her eyes widened.

She didn't think about her mother much in the day. She was too busy rushing down to school or climbing back hungry for lunch. It was while lying in bed that the memories came.

Fore dey mudda leave, dey did hav Christmas decorations in a store in town. Not every store, jus one. So dey mudda di' say: "Paper chain an a paper bell, *oui*. Long fore dey time…"

Having returned from the market, her mother had stood motionless talking to someone out in the street. This was when they lived in the long wooden house, two streets away from the businesses in town. The hillside house and its hanging entry porch now lit up in Wheeler's mind.

Dey mudda di' stay outside on d'porch, holding onta she messages. Talking bout Christmas. She in know who she mudda talking to.

Slow, pitying tears rolled down Wheeler's face.

Adele had taken their mother's bags away from her and carried them into the house.

"But Christmas in come yet. It not come yet," their mother had said.

By d'time it come f'decoration in all o' d'stores in town, dey mudda di' awready gone.

4

They walked everywhere, overlooked by layers of ledges and houses and roads rotating around the bay. With no bus service, without the means to pay in any case, they walked to church and to school. They even walked the mile or so on the rare occasion they went to town – a distance made longer by the circling roads.

On the way to school, Wheeler glanced up at Adele, hoping she might slow down.

Wheeler returned her eyes to the ground.

The shadows of breadfruit and banana branches fell like discarded limbs across the surface of the road. Wheeler started thinking about her mother. Not the one that had stayed out on the porch talking about decorations in town, but the mother who had taken extra care of her because she was still young. The mother that had told them they should look out for one another when she was gone, and not fall out. Wheeler wanted to tell that mother about Hesta.

How she does cut her off when she try an talk. Styling her off, jus so, f'nutting at all. How Hesta acting big now.

She di' warnt she mudda t'come back and warn d'two o' dem t'take good care of her.

She took a deep breath and sped up.

And she di' warnt her t'warn Adele. T'tell her: she hav t'leave f'school on time an stop making dem run.

Though they had caught up to the early children ahead of them, still Adele maintained a frantic pace. She hurried past the row houses, their backs high above the deep cinema yard. The outline of the makeshift rum shop beckoned at the turn. A marker on the way to school, no matter what they'd left behind there was no turning back, once they reached the rum shop.

Wheeler frowned at Adele. Her hair was swept up again today.

At the corner, a group of younger girls going arm in arm fixed their eyes on Adele. A set of whispering eyes and long looks. Adele appeared to be ignoring them.

Gyuls wearing d'*same* blue an white tie like she sister. Gyuls from she sister school.

From time to time other girls would nod to Adele and say, "Y'okay?" and her sister would nod back. But this wasn't like that.

Dey *looking*… like dey in see Adele before!

Wheeler didn't ask why.

She in warnt she sister stopping her in d'street and cutting style on her again.

Wheeler picked up her pace, started trotting – quick,

28

short steps.

Further along from the rum shop, small A-frame houses lined the street, surrounded by low pawpaw and heavy breadfruit trees. A slow-coming car eased along Russell Street to Adele and Wheeler's rear, nudging layers of children aside.

"Mind yerself." Adele slowed down. She steered Wheeler to the shallow drain on the side of the shoulderless road.

Wheeler frowned at Adele, then at the two-toned Austin as it approached.

There was next to no vehicle traffic on Russell Street before the junction leading up from Wharf Road. Children and grown people made that stretch of the street their own. The driver tutted his horn at the stragglers further on who seemed reluctant to get out of the way.

Climbing up from the drain, Wheeler spotted an unexpected picture of the family house on a distant ledge between the street and the sky.

"Wha y'looking at?"

A corner of the roof and the side veranda gazed down at her.

5

Long lazy slopes fell down to the shore, some in afternoon sun, others draped in shadows. The following week, climbing the Cut, Wheeler looked back. She lowered her eyes towards Russell Street.

She di' living in a place whey… whoever di' warnt could jus see her! Wedda she up on d'lane or else down dere.

A place with more steps compared to town – one hundred and sixty-three in all, from the bottom of the Cut to the top.

They had started climbing the fifty-three steps from the veranda entrance together. Now Donelle stretched ahead of her. Goatweed and tall brittle grass bounded the un-railed stairway to her side. The higher Wheeler went, the more fretful she became.

Even d'water in look d'same!

Tilting forward, supported by an upper step, Wheeler stared down through her legs into the distance. Upside-down buildings crowded the headland. The water had disappeared altogether. Roofs turned to brick to grass as she straightened up.

A giant shoe print, St Catherine's Bay was far removed

from the vast wilderness on the edge of town, a wilderness of indigo, violet and rarest blue. Long-distance ships would materialise, waver and change course out on the horizon. What she once knew had been taken away from her. A never-ending sea, replaced by the hemmed-in basin below.

Wheeler lifted her leg over the kerb, wobbling a little. The distance between her and Donelle had extended. "Wait, na!" she cried out. "Dey not starting yet!"

Part way up the lane, Donelle stopped. He'd been heading towards a large building at the height of the spur.

'Sif he in hav nutting better t'do.

His body seemed to slacken. He drifted back to her.

Wheeler looked to the upper part of the building, visible above a concrete wall.

He di' jus take off when she say bout going.

Situated inside a walled enclosure, the hurricane assembly hall was constructed years ago after a devastating storm. It was now a place for the weekly Girl Guide meeting. They were going up to peek their heads inside the hall with the Guide group still in there. Although this had been Wheeler's idea to begin with, she was no longer sure it was something she wanted to do. She dipped her head and stalled, gazing down at her dress.

Dey jus wearing dey homeclothes, dey in wearing dey good clothes. Okay if dey jus running up an down d'place. Not if dey going up t'd'Guide Hall door.

Donelle gestured to her: *C'mon.*

Wheeler made her way to him, forcing herself to move on.

She dint warnt t'get in trouble wid she sisters again. She sisters di' start getting close – troubling her bout everyting now dey mudda gone. Whey Adele di' always go t'Guides by sheself, now Hesta di' start going too.

"Y'ready?"

The spectre of Hesta, hands on her hips, reared up at Wheeler off the cracked surface of the road. Her legs weakened. At the perimeter wall, her afternoon shadow cowered at her side. Tiny maggots wriggled in her stomach, the kind she'd seen crawling inside dead crapeau and snakes stinking on the side of the road. Squaring off at the turn, the line of the hurricane hall followed the lane's gentle downward roll.

Donelle sauntered past the opening in the wall as if taking a harmless stroll, his shirt front dangling on a single button. "Okay?"

Was not okay…

Wheeler gave him a pained look. She kept her thoughts to herself.

She in warnt him tinking she di' fraid. Fraid o' wha she sisters go do if dey catch her interfering wid dey meeting.

The entrance to the hall was situated a good way from them, over a concrete walkway. The storm shutters and heavy wooden door had been thrown wide open, revealing the building's pale green walls and brown ceiling beams. The bell tower was empty, no bell to warn of an impending storm.

Donelle stared across at the open door. Wheeler twisted her face.

She in know how he could kerry on like he in worried.

She looked away from his crooked houseshirt.

A sudden eruption of emotion *whoosh*ed out of the building. Donelle pulled back. A list of names was being read out. Again the *whoosh* came, as the Girl Guides clapped.

Donelle strolled across to Wheeler's side. "Wait a minute fore we go," he said. "Dey jus now sitting down."

The maggots wriggling in Wheeler's stomach migrated and started nibbling at her behind. "Why we in jus go back?"

Having no recollection of how she had arrived there, Wheeler found herself crouching to the side of the Guide Hall door. Donelle smirked from the other side.

The *whooshing* inside the hall continued, louder now, up close. From where she crouched, Wheeler could see a section of the stage and a half-circle of girls.

No sign o' she sisters—

Donelle raised a finger to his lip and then gestured: *Look.*

The Guide leader, Miss Bench, strolled past the front of the stage.

Miss Bench?

Wheeler knew Miss Bench, a big-bosomed woman she saw in the churchyard on Sundays. Though she'd anticipated seeing Miss Bench, she became overwhelmed nonetheless upon *seeing* her. Married to the church organist, Miss Bench didn't like children. *Else dey keep dey mout shut an behave deyself.*

Wheeler's bewildered eyes drifted towards Donelle, finger still at his lip.

If Miss Bench di' tell he mudda dey bring deyself in d'Guide Hall, Tant'Innez would gi' d'two o' dem two lash.

A split second after Miss Bench went strolling past on her way to the back of the hall, Donelle flew past the open doorway. "Dat's showing Miss *Belch*!" he said.

Wheeler cupped her hand to her mouth, giggling. She and Donelle ran down the bank, slicing through the tall grass. As Wheeler ran, a small window slid open in her mind, a brief and dizzying opening.

Dey dint run everyting!

She realised there could be an escape from Miss Bench, an escape from her sisters and the way they'd had her thinking. At the perimeter wall she spun round and round to a drunken halt.

6

When Wheeler went down to the kitchen the following morning, her other aunt walked in, coming from the shower under the stairs.

A large, rubbery-looking woman, Innez had her nightie thrown around her neck and two bath towels covering her. Her hands clutched at the sides where the towels met. She was wearing a pair of eyeglasses, which she adjusted with the aid of a naked wet shoulder.

Part way down the stairs, Wheeler hesitated.

Tant'Innez di' giv her two lash on d'back o' she leg wid a belt. F'not sweeping d'yard. Four lash f'not bringing d'clothes off d'line when it still used to rain. She di' fraid she ant.

Innez approached. Wheeler shifted right. Innez shifted left. Wheeler found herself blocking the way.

Innez shook her upturned head. Her hard, brooding face reminded Wheeler of Floyd. "Why y'in look whey y'going?"

"Morning, Tantie Innez. Ah sorry, Tant'Innez."

Innez walked around her and climbed up the stairs.

Wheeler headed for the yard to see where Celeste was.

Celeste appeared at the end of the dark passageway underneath the stairs. Going out to the yard, she said, "Whey all-you bin after school yesterday?"

A question appeared on Wheeler's face: *Tant'Celeste di' know wha dey do?*

"Geraldine gone in d'country. She looking f'all-you. See if all-you warnt t'go."

Adele appeared, loaded down with books. "Tant'Celeste, we going!"

As Wheeler ran out of the house, she answered, "W-e… we jus playing. Up on d'lane."

Later, after school, Donelle and Wheeler set off round the top of the Cut. Going in the opposite direction to the Guide Hall, they made their way towards the dry grass slope. Donelle went first, shortpants fraying at the hem. Wheeler followed in a grey pinafore dress.

As she strolled round the corner, a vivid sense of her mother waylaid Wheeler, a memory of her bustling in the morning before leaving for work, her mother's swirling busyness somehow recreated on the hot breeze. Wheeler pictured her mother stooping and kissing her on the cheek. Catching her breath, she muttered to herself. "We mudda sending f'us."

"When she sending f'all-you?"

Wheeler stopped and looked up.

He dint usually say nutting when she talk bout she mudda.

"We mudda sending f'us," she said.

"When?"

"She sending f'us soon."

She dint know when.

The stony-faced buildings on the headland seemed to be following the cousins around. Donelle said, "Y'in tink we going f'a walk?"

Wheeler shook her head. "No, ah in tink we going." She stared at the ground. There was always something frightening in the night.

More fright'ning when people start telling ole-time story.

Wheeler frowned.

She di' tink he fraid o' night walk same as her.

They shimmied up the shoulder-high wall that was keeping a cone-shaped slope off the road and climbed a level higher, at which point the line of the wall disappeared below. Striding through the tickly grass, they headed towards a stand of cokey-o-co trees on the summit.

The noise of unseen crickets spiked the air. Feathery swishweed and needle grass combed Wheeler's legs. And everywhere the smell of seawater, familiar and natural as her own scent: hard and salty by midday, listless and waning towards the end of the day.

They had risen above the height of the headland opposite. The outside sea now appeared, rising into the sky with no trace of a horizon; the Caribbean Sea riding the air above the church tower, a mirage of solid blue.

Wheeler flicked at the long, crisp grass.

"Y'in tink she see us?"

Who?

For a moment she wondered who he meant. Her features took on a pensive look. "She in see us," she muttered.

Still, Wheeler began worrying about Miss Bench, started fretting about the mountain-sized heap of trouble they'd be in if the Guide leader had in fact seen them.

Even self dey dint go inside d'hall.

"She in move wid yer mudda?"

Coming behind in the yellow grass, Donelle responded: "Ah in tink so."

Even so, Wheeler thought his mother and Miss Bench might be friends. She worried about what her aunt might do if she learnt they'd been at the Girl Guide meeting. Her thoughts circled back round.

Wheeler returned to thinking about her own mother, who'd never hit her with a belt or even her hands. She recalled her mother's presence on the breeze and wondered if she lay awake at night thinking about her.

If she di' tinking bout her jus now?

Donelle called up. "Y'in warnta go again next week?"

A long section of the sea on the other side of the headland had turned purple.

Wheeler gazed out. "No. Ah in warnta go again."

7

Christmas came a few weeks after their mother's departure.

Christmas Eve Wheeler had gone shopping in town with her sisters and cousins. They had approached the centre of town from the top of George Street, the opposite side from the sisters' former home. Situated in a valley behind the headland, St Catherine's town was made up of a small grid of streets with a series of steep hillside roads tumbling to the sea wall on Water Street.

Wheeler had tried, but she could not locate the hillside house in the distant patchwork of buildings and roofs.

There was no traffic on the roads. A policewoman stood idling at the junction of George Street and Church Street. Crowds flooded the streets below. *Dey go soon get mash-up*, Wheeler told herself, glancing at her whitewashed Keds. Wearing her good clothes – though not her Sunday shoes – and muttering under her breath, she pressed herself into the afternoon crowd and was soon conveyed along by it.

"Hole on." Grabbing Wheeler's arm, Adele pulled her back. She stumbled towards Adele, clutching a rolled-up sack. The small burlap sack contained a red apple.

Bunched together, Donelle and Jonathan inched along beside the sisters, carrying rolled-up sacks of their own.

The single apple was Wheeler's first purchase of the day, bought in the refrigerated shop on her way round Wharf Road. The Christmas apple had come from where her mother had gone to, the same place from where her Christmas money had been sent. She was hoping to buy a box of Dixee crackers, a purple tin of Cadbury's chocolates, plus a packet of iced biscuits to add to the sack before she went home.

Small in the crowd, Wheeler glanced up at the pulsing life of St Catherine's town projected overhead in loud, indecipherable sounds. She had the sense of hundreds – *thousands* – of people trawling from street to street. Unable to see anything else, she scanned the faces above her head: long jaws and round chins, sweaty turning necks; the hot afternoon sky breaking in between them. She could not see the shop windows.The sidewalk and road seemed to have become one. Inching along, Wheeler wasn't sure her feet were touching the ground.

"All-you move. *Move.*" Reaching over Wheeler, Hesta steered Jonathan by his shoulder. Jonathan reached out and tapped Donelle. They pulled away from the flowing crowd and beached up on the sidewalk.

Wheeler looked to Donelle, then to Jonathan. She saw something of her sense of dislocation reflected in their faces.

"Wait here. We buying Cracker Jack!"

Wheeler watched as her sisters disappeared. *"St-ay!"* one of them said.

And there all three remained behind a curtain of children, heads down, staring into a display window. Moments later, Jonathan forced her, himself and Donelle to the front. Wheeler found herself gazing at a farmyard of little chickens and sheep and cows. There was a model train in the window weaving in and out and around a papier mâché landscape. Blue-grey hills and trees surrounded the farmyard animals.

She di' see a picture of a train in a book, but she in never see a train going round.

Wheeler stared at the animals in the field.

D'fowl and cow look like dey warnt t'see d'train, but dey carnt turn round.

A boy to her side pointed and turned and bumped his head against the glass.

Her sisters returned. "Come on. Open up y'bag."

A packet of Cracker Jack in each of their sacks. Wheeler's mouth sagged open. "But—"

"All-you getting d'same *ting*. Dat way all-you carnt argue," Hesta said.

"But," Wheeler argued, "ah warnt a tin of Cadbury's chocolate an a packet a ice biscuit!"

She di' like t'buy wha *she* warnt t'buy f'Christmas.

Donelle stepped in. "Least Floyd in come wid us."

Wheeler's eyes flared. "Sch-uu-pes!"

41

Floyd in no biznis o' hers.

"When ah getting m'chocolate?"

By the time they'd made their way to the Esplanade, the bright yellow afternoon had turned a paler shade. More people had piled themselves into town – people Adele and Hesta knew. They came to a halt.

Wheeler grew restless listening to her sisters talk to yet more of these girls.

Talking bout who dey di' see, whey dey di' go.

Shrinking to one side, Wheeler marvelled at the absence of her mother.

She missing Christmas!

The eddying crowd bumped up against Jonathan, Donelle and Wheeler as they waited for her sisters. Looking down past her Christmas sack, Wheeler could no longer see her feet or her whitewashed Keds.

"Okay, le' we go."

She rejigged the sack. A box of Dixee crackers had joined the red apple and the red and gold box of Cracker Jack. As they set off to purchase a packet of iced biscuits, Wheeler caught sight of the large paper bells her mother had worried about the month before.

"We not going in d'bookshop," Adele said.

Wheeler nodded, leaving behind the paper garlands connecting them to their mother.

They had their supper standing up in the bakery on

Back Street, eating bakes-n-souse, deep-fried balls of dough filled with saltfish, tomato and onions. They stood squashed together just inside the door. The sky was blue and black with a deep streak of red. A broken moon stuttered and quickened on the other side of the headland, when Wheeler looked out.

8

It was the custom to go walking at night, to leave front yards and side verandas and set off under a sunless sky. To feel a little cooler air against their skin.

Friday night they went for a walk.

Before leaving, Wheeler and Donelle sat up on the veranda waiting for Adele and Hesta to come out. The final traces of daylight had given up an hour earlier, the remnants of twilight fading with the coming of the night. Now blackness covered the land like a state order: a thin scattering of lamplight and candlelight marked out the remoteness of the steep, circling slopes. Lower down, around the waterfront, red, yellow and blue lines squiggled on the water from the shop windows around Wharf Road.

The sounds of the animal night ushered up from the ground, a sound as ancient as the earth: the incessant chirps of crickets, of electric mobs of insects; the unnerving shrill of mongoose rising from wild places surrounding the house.

Remaining on the safe shore of the veranda, Donelle and Wheeler both glanced at one another as if seeking the reassuring presence of the other.

She di' *know* he di' fraid.

They were afraid of all the spirits of the night, any of whose call might be disguised in the frenzied chatter all around: afraid of ligaroo and jumbie, of lajablesse, the hoof-footed temptress, whose long flowing dress concealed the terrible truth of what she was!

Two shadows installed themselves at the front of the house, under Wheeler and Donelle. Tipping forward, getting closer to one another, the cousins looked down on them: blurry manifestations imprinted on the night. One of them spoke in the voice of Adele: "Come on. Le' we go!"

"Whey we going?"

"We going round by d'lane."

Donelle and Wheeler ran out.

Sweet night air enveloped them as they descended towards her sisters. Emboldened by their presence, Wheeler squeezed past and took off down the Cut. They were taking the long way round to the road above.

Donelle followed Wheeler and shoved her. They started fooling, pushing one another up and down the invisible steps.

"All-you stop!"

Wheeler searched in the dark for her sisters, but was unable to find them.

"Whey Jonaton?" Donelle said, seeming now to be enjoying himself.

"He musta gone down awready."

On the level below, disembodied voices greeted them from inside an unseeable world. "Evening."

Donelle and Wheeler carried on to where the ledge of little semi-dark houses ended, to the point where the flow of jagged steps returned.

The week before, a woman from one of the houses had come to the kitchen door, begging Celeste for sticks of cocoa tea, and Wheeler had stood there listening. Poor as they were, as the woman had started leaving, she'd heard her aunt say, "Come! Take a chunk o' tania as well – do."

At the bottom of the Cut, Wheeler's eyes darted towards a light on the cinema building. There was a filmshow on. Distant figures hung around the open cinema gate. Others brushed past on their way down into the yard. Waiting beside Donelle, she watched them.

D'gate di' close when she di' warnt t'go by d'bread shop.

Wheeler searched the bank on the edge of the road. She couldn't see Jonathan.

"All-you come."

She and Donelle strolled on after her sisters. The rattle of small rocks like trinkets under their feet as they climbed the roadside track. A buttress wall rose to their left, with the lights of a row of houses above. The creak of running water came from an overhead drain. Long slanted shadows moved inside the weatherboard houses quivering in candlelight.

The route to the lane ran through a grove of dried banana stems, where the row of houses ended.

Wheeler swung round. Something had started following them along the crunching stones and rocks. Her sisters had stretched ahead. Wheeler touched Donelle's side and pointed. Donelle ran away, the soles of his flip-flops crackling over the track.

A voice returned from the past: *Leave her!*

Wheeler stood still.

She mudda di' say "Leave her" when dey di' go walking one night. She in know *who*, she in know *what* she mudda di' tell. She in never feel fraid when she mudda di' dere.

"Jonaton!" Wheeler exhaled. Jonathan and some other boys were walking through the dim beam of light beneath the final house. She watched them disappear as darkness reclaimed them.

Suspended between the two groups, Wheeler floundered.

Donelle an dem di' go inside d'bush awready, dey in wait. Jonathan an dem, dey still coming.

On hearing the joking figures draw near, Wheeler started moving, mapping a path between the trunk-like banana stems, her two arms extended. Wild cocoa trees began to appear, a handful of them to her left; their copper-tinted leaves gave off an iridescence. She trampled deeper into the grove moving in time to the teenagers shuffling at the back, not getting too far ahead of them.

"Why she in go wid Donelle an dem?"

"Hush up," someone said.

Half-listening to their overlapping voices, Wheeler

47

remained alert. She gave her full attention to the nearby cocoa pod heads, the upright bodies of the banana stumps – gave her attention to the night spirits instead.

A jumbie might still be hiding heself. Might still walk out an grab her! Ne'er mind she here wid Jonaton an dem.

The overgrown banana grove ended at a low turntable, with the top lane angled overhead. There on the level ground the nightwalkers would pause, with someone telling an old-time story. The group would then tackle the climb to the lane.

Wheeler's feet stumbled against the rock-hard ground, after the final banana stump.

"Whey y'bin?" Hesta's judgemental voice.

Later that night, lying in bed, Wheeler thought about the last time she'd seen her mother. It was in the sitting room to the back of where she lay now. She shifted her head on the pillow, unable to make sense of her mother having been in the house, unable to reconcile that memory with her not being there now.

She mudda di' *right here* talking t'Tantie Innez.

Wheeler's lips quivered.

Both women had stood a curt distance apart in the sombre light of the sitting room. "Well, if y'warnta go…" said Innez, with Wheeler watching them.

She mudda di' look like she di' warnt t'cry.

Their mother had swivelled around as Adele came into

the room.

Hair pinned up, wearing her church dress, their mother had pressed her lips together and taken a deep breath.

"C'mon," Adele had told Wheeler, "le' we go up an look at d'ship."

The expression on her mother's face was of no account to Wheeler as she walked out to the veranda. But that look would return to her over the coming days. It came back to her now. She recalled her mother looking like she herself sometimes did: attempting to appear brave when she wasn't feeling that way.

"Why y'going? Why ah carnt come?" she'd asked, having come back from staring at the ship.

"We-ll, it busy an dark down dere," her mother had said, as if about to leave. "Is better y'in come—"

"But ah warnt t'come wid you in *Ingland*!"

A sickened look appeared on their mother's face. She had gestured to Adele and Hesta with a despairing shake of her head.

Why she di' shake she head?

Their mother then took the older girls' faces to either side of hers. "Time'll soon come," she said. "Ah sending f'all-you soon."

But time in soon come, like she mudda di' say!

9

The dock was empty the following day, as was the wide-open entrance to the bay. Late morning, a long-mouthed schooner could be seen berthed in front of the lumberyard. There were passengers waiting to take the ship to the neighbouring island. Wheeler stood part way up the Cut, waiting for her mother to come out.

She di' never see she mudda going away from d'house.

The night of their mother's departure, her sisters had grabbed Wheeler as she ran towards the veranda chasing after their mother; had held her back as she hopped and howled.

The long veranda was in part-shade, light tilted across the terraced garden. Wheeler's mind wrestled with light and shade, with night and day. Her bewildered eyes bounced from the terraced yard to the veranda. She was unable to picture her mother's departure, by day or by night.

"Y'in see dem?"

Past and present splintered at the sound of Donelle's voice. She let the thought of her mother fall out of her mind.

"Y'in see whey dey deh?" Donelle called again from the bottom entrance.

Wheeler looked away from the shrivelled bloodroot stems, the crispy black-eyed vines choking the garden, to where Wharf Road emerged from under the cover of the land. She shook her head. "Ah in see dem." Moments later, as she neared the top, as Donelle approached, she gestured. "Dey dere."

A faraway image appeared of Jonathan and Adele advancing along Wharf Road. Her sister and Jonathan were out buying messages. Donelle had made his brother promise to buy a packet of Chiclets for him and Wheeler to share if there was any money left over.

As if suspecting what she was thinking, Donelle gave Wheeler a side-on look. "Y'in tink he goan buy it?"

Wheeler frowned. She shook her head.

She in know.

Saturdays there was always something going on, everyone getting their work done. There was sweeping and washing. Mornings there was buying messages. Afternoons the baking got done.

She sister di' put on she pink shirt an nice green skirt f'going in d'shop.

Adele and Jonathan would head back down to the market after coming home. They couldn't carry all the messages at once.

Donelle and Wheeler suited themselves all day Saturday,

nobody interested in them once they got their chores done. She had washed her sisters' school Keds and her own, had pegged all six to the clothesline by their canvas tongues. Had pegged them up still dripping – with Hesta watching her from the lower yard. Wheeler had then swept the yard on the furthest side of the house while Donelle swept and tidied up Floyd's bedroom. After returning the yard broom, she had run away up the Cut before Hesta or anyone else could find something else for her to do.

Part way up the lane, Wheeler looked round. Donelle was still standing where she'd left him. Taking pity on him, she yelled down: "Maybe dey can still hav some money left over," she said, though without much conviction.

As if waiting for this assurance, Donelle started coming uphill. Wheeler walked on, not waiting.

The night before, with the two walking parties coming together, Jonathan had gotten in trouble with Adele.

One o' he fren di' start telling a story bout a ligaroo over on Carter Hill, when dey siddown under d'lane.

"Man look jus like you and me in d'day. Hgh, when night come, man turn into a big ole flappy bird."

At that point her deep mistrust of the night had resurfaced, the sense of the twitching, restless night being outside all their control. Wheeler had wanted to run home but could not remember how, could not move.

"Man fly in over on Carter Hill an suck a woman in she—"

"Bwoy, why y'in hush up!" Adele di' tell him. "Eh-eh, y'in see m'little sister sitting right dere?"

He di' stop talking den.

"And as f'*you*," Adele di' tell Jonaton, "how y'ain self *tink* bout yer own brudda as well?"

Jonaton di' swing way from d'bwoy. "Ah in tell him say dat—"

Wheeler paused, reaching the top of the lane.

Jonaton di' seem worried, 'sif he tink she sister go tell Tant'Innez when dey get home. Adele woulnt do dat.

Looking back over the terrain – over the length of the headland and the water – Wheeler could no longer see Wharf Road. She could no longer see Adele or Jonathan.

In the afternoon, with a brilliant display of silver water at their backs, Donelle and Wheeler scaled the rocky kitchen yard.

"Whey all-you going?" Jonathan asked them. He was sitting at the back of the house on the gutter ledge, playing a game of marbles with a teenage boy, Bounce.

Donelle answered, "We jus going up d'Cut."

Slipping past Donelle, Wheeler went and sat down beside Jonathan. "Dey still baking," she said, "we jus come f'sumting t'eat." The bread and coconut buns were still in the oven. There'd be nothing to eat until supper.

"Eh-eh! All-you come up make me lose meh concentration?" said Bounce.

A gentle, sneaky grin from Jonathan. "Thankya, Bounce." Standing up, pockets jingling, Jonathan produced a red-eyed shooter from his pocket, knelt to the ground and took his turn. He lined up his shot, eyes moving from his thumb then back as he aimed.

Heels in the gutter, chins on their knees, Wheeler and Donelle watched.

Half on his knees, half-twisted, Jonathan launched his glass shooter at the spray of marbles. Again. And again, sweeping up the field.

"See wha all-you do?" Bounce lurched forward, his eyes taking on a wild and threatening look.

Wheeler gazed at Bounce: his small neat ears, the g-r-rumphy screwed-up expression on his face. She sat back, unconcerned.

E'rybody know how Bounce do.

"Okay. One more time," Bounce urged, jerking his bony head. He and Jonathan laid down an equal number of marbles on the ground.

Jonathan's aim slipped—

Bounce's turn.

They switched back and forth.

Another game lost.

Bounce demanded another try.

As the sparring continued, blunt afternoon heat rose up off the ground, smited Wheeler's face. An involuntary stupor descended over her. Almost asleep, she nodded herself awake. Floyd was looking down at them from his bedroom window.

Saturday, half-day closing. A carpenter – apprenticed to Old Man Guppy by the cemetery gate – Floyd had returned home from work. He glared out of the window, muscular arms bulging from his short-sleeved shirt. "Ah taut ah tell you stay way from dis yard?"

Jonathan's head swung round.

Floyd had his eyes on Bounce.

Bounce at first ignored Floyd, intent on the game. His long, square back remained contorted where he lay curled on the ground. Then he kissed his teeth: "Sc-h. Man, wha y'causing confusion for?"

Floyd's head then his torso flew out the bedroom window. The frame struggled to contain him—

"Warnt ah put meh *foot* in yer arse?"

Donelle fled. Wheeler stared after him. She stood up, started making her way towards the Cut.

Bounce uncurled himself and looked up. "Okay, okay…" He held up his hand. He started separating out his marbles.

Floyd said, "Get d'h-ell outa here!"

"Aw-right."

Wheeler watched as, clutching the marbles in one hand, Bounce stumbled to his feet and hauled up the seat of his shortpants. "Ah going—"

"*Ma*-co!" she heard Floyd yell.

Climbing the Cut, Wheeler watched Bounce's narrow, pointed head sink deeper and deeper below her. Meanwhile, Donelle had hastened uphill and was waiting for her to the side of the lane. His blank eyes were fixed on the view.

"Why he in like Bounce?" she asked him.

Donelle lowered his head.

Bounce was always joking about. "In nobody in like Bounce," she said.

Donelle lowered his head a notch more, something she'd seen him do before telling what he knew.

He di' drop he head fore saying how Floyd di' rap he an Jonaton cross dey head.

Wheeler sat down waiting on Donelle.

He shook his head. "Ah in know."

They wandered around the corner with the bay to their right, a hot gleaming eye at the centre of the terrain. The lane levelled out before them and then dropped. They scaled the roadside wall to their left.

Donelle got ahead of Wheeler on the overhead slope. He shouted back something she didn't hear.

A solitary motor car trawled the crawl space opposite in between the terraces. Its signalling chromework caught her eye. Wheeler looked round. Rafts of trees and painted houses inched along the hillsides on the way round to where she stood, including along Clarkton Road, where she and Donelle went to school.

Wheeler's eyes lighted on a section of Mill Street further

down. She looked away from the Methodist church to Mill Street's other end, to where Donelle had once pointed.

He di' point out d'house whey he farda live – his an Jonaton. Floyd hav a diffrent farda from dem.

Carrying on up, she went and joined Donelle where he sat under the cokey-o-co trees. "Is true. Is tree weeks til kite season," he repeated. "Den carnival."

Now she di' know wha he di' saying before.

She hadn't heard him on the way up. Eyes to the ground, acclimatising to the shade, Wheeler thought about what he'd said.

"Is true," Donelle insisted. "Is tree weeks til kite season come. Den come carnival."

A hint of resistance came into Wheeler's face.

She might'n know when kite season come, but she dint tink he know heself.

They stretched out on their backs underneath the cokey-o-co's slim, overlapping branches. The vast translucent sky peeped in at them with eyes of blue – the same sky in every peek, though not the same blue.

10

One quiet morning in the middle of January, Wheeler awoke early, alert, as if summoned. Sea water eddied and reflected on the tongue-and-groove ceiling. She sat up, and, kneeling over Adele's sleeping body, reached for the side window. Creeping around the cliff where the headland ended, the glowing white prow of the banana boat slipped into view.

Wheeler shrank back.

She mudda di' go in Ingland on d'banana boat.

A new year. The ship's first arrival since her mother's departure. A blast of the ship's horn—

"Ur-gh." Adele pushed Wheeler away.

Striding over Hesta, Wheeler tumbled to the bedroom floor, out of the room, and felt her way down the creaking kitchen stairs. At the middle landing, she hesitated. She recalled seeing the ship before its departure.

That evening, leaving the house with Adele, she had climbed the hillside steps with a growing sense of adventure.

Wha she seeing?

Wheeler's feelings of excitement had soon turned to confusion as she saw what lurked in the harbour: a long sliver of white caught under the cover of the trees and the land. Stout, charred funnels. Black and white. A large seagoing ship moored to the side of the bay.

D'ting dat d'come t'take she mudda away!

Blood had knocked at Wheeler's temples, sharp and loud. She and Adele had met Hesta part way up. Not staying long, her sisters had headed back to the house.

She dint warnt t'go back in d'house. She di' warnt t'go wid she mudda in Ingland!

"Y'not coming back down?"

Wheeler had looked round to find her cousin, Donelle.

She remembered him standing beside her. She hadn't seen him come up.

Now, eyes quickening, she went down the stairs and out into the yard as the banana boat approached: a reminder of her mother – more brutal than a Christmas paper chain.

The ship's prow pointed at the harbour like a primed weapon. A tugboat glided port side. Puffs of black smoke belched into the still morning air.

Too early even for Celeste, Wheeler stood alone on the edge of the retaining wall in her thin nightdress.

Carrying a cargo of bananas and passengers from neighbouring islands, all bound for England, the freighter nosed its way towards the harbour. The letters *G.E.E.S.T* emblazoned along its hull, the ship came fully into view, blocking the mouth of the bay as the last of it edged around the cliff. The tiny figures on the tug watched it go.

The memory of her mother's departure overwhelmed her.

How she inside could pain so?

Wheeler looked away.

Celeste appeared, tying together her housedress.

Wheeler's eyes implored Celeste, as if to say *Look*! "I-t come back," she muttered as Celeste nudged her into the house and settled her on a kitchen stool.

Celeste looked off to the sink window, still straightening her clothes. "It goan keep coming back," she said as if to herself. A length of string fastened around her meagre waist, she went back out into the yard.

Her small ribcage contracting, Wheeler stayed where she'd been placed by Celeste. The uneasy stillness of the morning was soon cut through by the sounds of the feeding chickens chuckling out in the yard. She could no longer see the banana boat as it continued to dock. She gazed across the counter to the headland. Coconut trees glistened here and there, their upheld branches like static windmill blades. Wheeler's eyes fell to the shore.

Two vehicles made their way around: one a red and white van – white on top, red at the bottom. The distance was such that she saw them in miniature. She was sometimes able to make out people she knew as they made their way round. But there wasn't anyone walking along now.

All day long, little country trucks would bump their way around Wharf Road heaped with green bananas, on their way to the port. Then later that night, somebody's brother, sister, father – someone else's mother would carry luggage to the harbour and climb the gangway to be carried away by the banana boat.

Celeste returned with the feed bucket, which now contained the breakfast eggs. The noise in the yard started to die down. "Dry yer eyes."

Doing as her aunt said, Wheeler pressed the back of her hands against her eyes. She focused on the rusted head of the kitchen tap so she wouldn't look out of the side window by accident.

She dint warnt t'see d'boat.

"Y'does help yer mudda?"

"Sometimes," Wheeler answered, eyelashes smudged though no longer wet.

"Gi' me a hand do, an swizzle dese eggs."

Kneeling up on the uneven stool, Wheeler watched as Celeste cracked egg after egg into an enamel basin. She started counting part way through, not having seen so many eggs being cracked open before.

"Ge' a swizzle stick."

Wheeler reached for one of a number of wooden implements inside a copper jug.

Hugging the basin against her chest, Celeste rejected the thin swizzle stick and selected another one, still carrying on cracking the eggs. "Jus hole on. So."

Wheeler started rubbing the blackened swizzle stick

between her palms, slicing into the buttery yolks with the eager, claw-like foot. Celeste's roughened, veined hands held on to the bowl.

When it came, the noise from the ship's anchor chain echoed around the terraces circling the bay. Wheeler's head lifted. Buildings to the left and right of the Anglican clock tower appeared to tremble.

"D'boat come back," she said.

Her two sisters were out of bed. Eyebrow cocked, Hesta glanced at Adele. There were tears in Wheeler's voice, smears of it still on her face.

"Whey y'bin?" asked Adele.

"In d'kitchen, talking t'Tantie Celeste."

Hesta grabbed her bath towel and walked out of the room.

"Why y'troubling Celeste?" Adele said.

"Ah in troubling her." Wheeler lolled onto the bed, eyes rolling towards the side window. "Ah jus seeing how d'boat come back, how it come... Ah jus seeing it." She sat up. "An Tant'Celeste try t'help."

"Don't trouble Celeste," Adele said. "Get yerself ready f'school."

11

The following morning, blue sunlight spread across the headland in pale, milky rays. A softer beginning than the day before. An early van drove away to the left, on the edge of the wide windows. The clear, white water of the bay appeared calm and forgiving after the ructions of the previous day.

Unsettling memories came to mind: the long white boat, drifting clouds of smoke. The anchor's rattling echo and the warning of her sisters afterwards.

Don't trouble Celeste.

Despite her sister's warning, Wheeler had come down again.

Dey in know how d'boat di' make her feel. It di' bring back all d'bad feelings from when she mudda di' run out, leaving. Dey upstairs in dey bed – dey in see!

Wheeler swizzled the eggs with swift resentment.

Dey in watch d'boat coming in. Tant'Celeste di' see. She di' stop her worrying. Did leave she mind at ease.

Celeste had given Wheeler the eggs to mix today, unaided. The dozen or so eggs were already frothing.

Wheeler drew the basin closer and harder against her chest. She didn't want the basin to slip.

She ant might take it way.

A tender transition seemed to have taken place in Celeste. Wheeler had sensed the change. Standing beside her, Celeste started making the cocoa tea. She took a stick of field cacao from a tin – more branch than stick. The thick cacao roll was a bitter, rich brown, redolent of the texture and flavour of their mealtime drink. Celeste crunched through the hardened cacao with a carving knife, scooped slices and crumbs into a cocoa pot. Threw a flick of orange peel and cinnamon into the tall metal pot.

"Dey in hav no boat out dere today," said Wheeler, having seen nothing in the harbour on her way down. The banana boat had sailed the night before.

Standing the cocoa pot under the tap, Celeste glanced out. "Is so things does go. It in hav much boat coming now. Dem ting done," she muttered. "Times hard. Y'in see the same kinda ship an vessel like before. Time was dey hav trawling ship an merchant ship, loading on d'docks. All kinda work f'people t'do…" Celeste's voice tailed off.

"We farda used t'work on d'docks."

Celeste looked the other way.

Her aunt's words rolled on in Wheeler's mind. *Trawling ship an merchant ship.* The view from the porch of her old home had been a vast picture of the Caribbean Sea stretching from the bottom of the road to the horizon. Now and then cruise ships and long merchant ships would cut across between Water Street and the horizon. Now and then on their way round to the port. But not often.

Celeste struck a match. Brow furrowing, she struck another one. She ignited the kerosene burner – *Phum!* – and threw both spent matches into the sink. The smell of burning kerosene stomped around the room.

With no mention of Wheeler's father, Celeste said, "Don't worry, all-you mudda goan send f'all-you." Then, checking inside the basin, she nodded. "Yea, dat look good."

A shy smile parted Wheeler's lips. It was as if Celeste had reached out and hugged her. In all the time she'd been in the house she had not felt any warmth from her aunt, who often just seemed tired and fed up.

The day before, Wheeler had heard Celeste tell Jonathan to take the kerosene inside the house. Jonathan had been joking with Hesta and Adele in the yard after coming back from the shop. Wheeler had watched Celeste take the kerosene can away and carry it into the kitchen, a long-suffering look on her face. She'd then watched Jonathan attempt to involve Celeste.

He di' try an giv dey ant d'joke so she could laugh wid dem. But she di' go in. Now, tho, she diffrent.

It seemed to Wheeler that Celeste might now stop and laugh with Jonathan.

She in never hear dey ant laugh, but one time she di' see her smile.

Wheeler had watched Celeste lift her lean chin into the air and break off shucking at the juking board with a broad smile. The smile had gotten bigger, broader as Celeste turned her gaze to the side of the house.

S'tho Tant'Celeste di' see sumting dere. Maybe she di' see she dead baby.

Glancing round from the stove, Celeste said: "Is time y'get y'bath towel an go in d'shower, fore e'rybody wake up." She had already taken away the basin of eggs.

Wheeler slipped down off the shaking stool. At the stairs, she said, "Tho we mudda gone, is not the same 'sif she dead."

A harrowing web seemed to spring up, covering Celeste's face. Scratching her arm, she looked away.

12

On her way to school two days later, Wheeler thought about her new-found friendship with Celeste. She realised it was what she'd always wanted.

She ant di' treat people rough. She di' tink she in care, but she di' care. Tant'Celeste baby did die when it little. She di' un'erstand bout sorrow more dan udda people.

Wheeler gave Adele a side-eyed look. She had continued going to the kitchen each morning, despite the banana boat's departure, despite the warnings from her sister.

This morning, as she knelt at the kitchen counter, there had been a weighty crack along the kitchen stairs. Wheeler's head had swung round. A broken-open sound was followed by Innez's shambling shadow near the top of the stairs. Wearing an oversized nightdress, Innez came struggling down, planting one hefty foot in front of the other. She glared at Celeste's back from the stairs.

Tant'Innez di' hav d'same vex look every time she look at Tant'Celeste.

Wheeler sensed there was something wrong between

them, though she had never heard them quarrel. Her eyes roamed from aunt to aunt. She couldn't figure out what was wrong. "Dey bin living together too long!" was all Adele had said.

She ant di' stay way from one anudda.

They spent their time in separate parts of the house: Celeste on the ground floor, Innez in her bedroom upstairs.

"Morn-ing, Tant'Innez."

No answer for Wheeler.

"Mor-ning."

"Morr-ning." The two women greeted one another.

Celeste kept on working, chopping cive and thyme, not turning round. Meanwhile, Innez cut across to the understairs toilet, but not before catching Wheeler looking at her. "Go upstairs an get y'bath towel," she said.

Wheeler had clattered backwards off the stool and hurried upstairs.

Now, stomping through a hodgepodge of shadows on Russell Street, she hopped to keep up with Adele. As they emerged from the shade, the flourish of a single steel pan startled the morning air. A lone figure stood in the distant band pit practising rapid calypso riffs.

The night she had walked out to the bread shop, Wheeler's mind had been hushed by the strangeness of standing at sea level. The gnawing of the sea, ravenous on the underside of the road, grew stronger and louder the closer she got. The pleated, golden waves broke away in the light. Lifting her eyes to the glowing rafters, she had felt herself reduced to the size of nothing.

Late afternoon. Wheeler climbed the slope at the side of the lane a little ahead of Donelle. At the summit, she trampled the fallen blossoms beneath the cokey-o-co trees.

Another January day with an unchanging sky, the clear canvas of blue covered over by an influx of thin popcorn cloud starting at the horizon. The breeze off the sea unhurried and dry, the clouds unmoving. No sign of rain.

The hem of her pinafore dress riding high, Wheeler approached the row of bushes beyond the twisted branches of the cokey-o-co shade, with Donelle close behind. Disappearing through the dense thicket, they headed for the back lane.

There were stray ears of corn and frail vines caught up in the shoulder-high bushes. The puffs of popcorn cloud, like the sunken waterfront, were now distant news at Wheeler and Donelle's backs. She picked her way through, pulling aside curtains of wily scratchy branches. Donelle had pushed on, bludgeoning the packed vegetation with a stick.

Wheeler's eyes dropped to the green and brown tangle at her feet.

"Jonaton di' say dey ain hav snake in here." She shook her head, whispering. "Dey ain in here. Dey like tick juicy grass like d'far side o' d'house—"

Wheeler carried on to the sinking side of the slope, her

eyes at first not accepting what they were seeing. Donelle lay head first, part way down, sketched in shadow underneath the indifferent trees, their giant canopies sheltering the back slope.

She rushed down. "Donelle."

He took a raw intake of air, then whimpered as he exhaled.

"Wha happen?"

Eyes brimming Donelle recoiled, as if to say *Y'carnt see wha happen*? He rolled onto his back. There was blood running down his leg. Rivulets collecting and rolling in the dark afternoon shade.

Gathering herself, Wheeler glanced uphill to where afternoon light struggled to make headway between the heavy trunks of the trees.

He musta trip and keep falling.

"Y'in fall so hard," she told him.

The grimace on Donelle's face said that he disagreed. He pushed himself up on his elbows. Wheeler squatted down beside him. Small, quick-fire birds crackled and twittered in the tangled branches above.

"Ah hav a scratch too." Wheeler stretched out her arm. She watched the disbelief develop in Donelle's eyes as he examined the vague mark.

They sat. The shadow of the lower branches reflected on Donelle's thin body and across his ragged shortpants, already torn before the fall. The blood kept on coming.

"Y'okay?"

Donelle looked away and shook his head.

There was a wide open basin in the distance below; the busy sound of activity rose between the trees. There was a rooftop on the underside of the lane. A little car sat on the edge of a driveway.

Wheeler looked at Donelle, his features deflated, a thoughtful look in his eyes. She looked away at the hollow below the lane, waiting for him to get his second wind.

They kept on waiting, not seeking help, unused to thinking that way.

Half an hour later, they made their way past the house on the underside of the lane with the little car in the driveway. They walked past, Donelle shuffling, Wheeler supporting him at times, to the sounds of children playing nearby.

Coming up to the fork in the road, the walls of the hurricane hall came into view where Villa Road met the lane. Veering left, the cousins followed the lane, past the bell tower entrance, over and then down the spur, with Donelle part-hopping the rest of the way.

Back in the yard, Donelle climbed into the concrete sink and turned on the tap. The side of his leg – a bloodied, matted mess – was studded with bits of twigs and dried leaves.

Coming in round the kitchen doorway, Wheeler said, "Donelle hut he leg."

Celeste sat on a stool by the counter, reading a paper.

She glanced up, turning her head halfway. "All-you bin by d'lane?"

Wheeler nodded. The seated figure did not get up.

Following Wheeler in, Donelle rested against the stove. Bloodstained water drained from the wound. Unable to remain standing, he hopped towards the stairwell. He straightened himself with the help of the stair posts as well as the rail.

Celeste watched Donelle shuffle up the stairs. The look on her face was fatalistic. Legs healed, week-old babies died, it seemed to say.

13

Two days on, the rip in Donelle's leg looked like an upside-down, rusted zip: dark nugget scar at the top with scabby interlocking teeth, set in a bloodless, yellow fluid. There was the occasional oozing of a clear liquid from between the teeth.

That afternoon, having climbed to the top of the Cut, Donelle followed Wheeler around the bend stiff-legged. Wharf Road curled around the bay, bleached and deserted, with businesses closed here until Monday and in town.

Donelle hoisted himself backwards onto the retaining wall, while Wheeler carried on up.

Jonathan and Adele had already made it back from the shops and the weekly market on Wharf Road. She had watched them unload the messages on their return.

Wheeler sighed.

Nutting nice. Dey di' buy bluggoe an tania. Saltfish, yeast and yam.

She gazed down at the top of Donelle's head.

Dey dint hav no change left over in dey hand – nutting f'a chewing gum f'she an Donelle t'chew.

The previous week, despite Donelle's hope and his desire, there had been no Chiclets bought either.

The sea appeared to the back of the church, distinct against the horizon. There was a blue-green house on the underside of the slope, its red split-level roof pressed open like the covers of a book. The only house up there, it sat two tiers above the now covered-over family house. A fat brown beetle landed on Wheeler's shin.

Flicking the beetle away, she strode on, grass licking at her naked legs.

The sound of a car on the lane. A light-coloured saloon came to a stop on the level crest of the lane, where nothing had been before. Wheeler stopped.

A man, then a woman, climbed out. They walked round to the boot from either side of the car. Tall, long and soundless, the man reached in for a bag, another bag, for two more. He placed them on the road. Straightening up, he lifted his arm and waved.

Donelle waved at their uncle and aunt – Morgan and Geraldine – returned from buying messages in town. He started shuffling downhill. Wheeler followed him. All four strolled away from the car and along the dip in the road, with Geraldine and Wheeler leading the way. Morgan carried two of the wicker bags with just one hand. With his other hand he balanced the contents of the remaining bag, hampered by Donelle's help.

They approached the blue-green house, Morgan and

Geraldine's home. The single storey house rose on the left-hand side of the lane. Tall concrete stilts and a stone wall kept the building and its surrounding garden off the road. Trimmed in white, the house shone in the afternoon sun.

Wheeler kept glancing back as she strolled downhill to the gate.

Dey uncle di' let Donelle help. D'spite o' he leg.

Empty-handed, she reached in front of her aunt and opened the iron gate. A concrete stairway climbed up to the side of the house, behind the tall metal gate. Morgan and Donelle approached with the shared shopping bag shifting between them.

She'd o' ask she uncle t' help. Woulda ask him but—

She did not know her aunt and uncle well. Wheeler had been taken to the house only once before her mother left. The weight of the gate made her arm bulge. Morgan placed his long body against the iron gate and kept it open.

Wheeler jumped on hearing the iron gate clang shut, as she followed Geraldine up the steps.

A mix of Innez and Celeste, Geraldine was slim like Celeste, though not suffering-looking. She was square-headed like Innez, though not threatening. "All-you hear from all-you mudda?" she asked. "Y'know how she getting on?"

"It still cold, she keep saying." Sweating in the unending heat, Wheeler had no sense how that might feel. "She say how she miss us. She still in say when she sending f'us."

Searching in her skirt pocket and producing a key, Geraldine said: "Yer mudda hav a lot she hav t'do. Everyting else okay?" Geraldine's voice was warm yet probing. "How y'sisters? Dey taking care o' you?"

Wheeler gave Geraldine a cautious look.

She sisters?

"Why y'still boddering Celeste?" Adele had asked the previous day. "Celeste ain yer mudda!" Hesta had warned her, joining in.

She sisters?... D'two o' dem does keep ganging up on her!

"Meh sisters... D'two o' dem dey fine, Tantie Geldine," answered Wheeler. Her eyes wandered around the room.

The kitchen was a pretty, colourful room with a tiled chessboard floor. The walls were a cushiony, soothing yellow with blue cupboard doors – tall cupboards on top, shorter cupboards below.

D'kitchen di' look please wid it niceness, like she di' sometimes feel in she church dress.

Wheeler's eyes landed on the box containers on the counter: SUGAR, FLOUR, RICE. No sack of flour under the counter, no stack of clanking cooking pots. Walking into the kitchen for the first time, Wheeler had been overawed by the sudden colours in the room, the diamond shapes on the floor.

"Y'like d'kitchen?" Geraldine had asked.

Wheeler had answered her aunt by nodding.

She mudda di' bring her by dem, when she was still little. Dat wha Tantie Geldine di' say.

But Wheeler didn't remember that time.

"Okay." Morgan hefted the messages onto the counter while Donelle waited in the doorway.

Wheeler went out and stood beside Donelle, looking regretful all over again, wishing she had offered to help as well.

"Y'warnt a drink?" Morgan had his eyes on Donelle as he spoke. Wheeler feared he might only be talking to him. "Ah go get all-you some mauby," he added.

Afterwards, walking home, Wheeler told Donelle, "Tant'Celeste di' say Tant'Geldine going in d'country. She di' looking f'us."

Glancing backwards, stumbling, Donelle sighed. "We can go anudda time."

14

Sunday morning, no cars at all, just people going to church. None of the usual bustle of schoolchildren.

Wheeler looked back, feet curling around one another, as she read the road.

Jus she sisters, plus anudda girl coming fardah back.

Having walked miles to and from school, most children attended church close to home.

Wheeler straightened round alongside Donelle and Jonathan. They'd already made it past the sagging rum shop. It was easy to miss without its usual clientele liming out on the porch. Beyond the A-frame houses, lazy water simmered and stirred, its yawning sound climbing up from Wharf Road.

At the centre of Russell Street they reached the Cable Street junction, from where waterfront traffic took a left on weekdays towards the police traffic box.

The cousins took the shortcut leading up to Mill Street. They climbed the fat concrete steps of the drain alley. All three were dressed in their Sunday clothes: the boys in crisp khaki shortpants and buttoned shirts; Wheeler wearing her pale gingham smock, a yellow ribbon in her hair; all of them wearing short white socks and church shoes. No Keds today.

Jammed between the walled-in houses, the storm drain carried rain and domestic water down to the sea. Its long, dry tongue could be seen in momentary gaps between the concrete treads. A church service was playing on a radio in one of the tall houses. Hearing the church organ's maddening rush, a dormant, anxious worm curled awake inside Wheeler's stomach. Her eyes tipped up in recognition: the "Children's March".

The week before Christmas, the boy behind Wheeler had tripped and crashed into her as they took part in the Sunday school procession, sending her forward into the slow-moving caravan of kids, who had just kept on tumbling.

She in cause it!

In no time the Sunday school teacher had responded to the wrecking of the procession by hauling Wheeler to the back of the line. The helter-skelter of the "Children's March" had scrambled on.

She di' put she hand on her… 'sif she know is she wha cause it!

The scorching sense of injustice remained – Wheeler could not bear to hear that music again. Eyes down, she climbed past Jonathan and Donelle, with Donelle limping a little.

On Mill Street they continued the long hike, stretching across the road in a single line.

The day before, Morgan had asked Donelle, "Wha happen t'yer leg?"

"Ah fall down," he'd said.

Morgan had enquired no further, had watched Donelle shuffle along the lane.

As they approached the church building, the Methodist church organ began playing, restrained and upright in contrast to that other time.

Turning into Churchway, they climbed the cobble steps, past the entrance to the church on their right.

Dey not going in dere!

They carried on to the elementary school, where the Sunday school classes met.

Eight o'clock, the walk almost at an end, Wheeler glanced back. Shoes clacking, a gaggle of churchgoers came hurrying up the alley, Hesta and Adele among them.

Wheeler stood in a classroom with other children, kids around her age, others younger than her – just like the Christmas procession; all of them waiting for the teacher to tell them to sit down. A U-shaped formation of benches and desks. Standing at the centre of the U, Wheeler listened to the heave of Jonathan and older children sitting down in the neighbouring room.

"Good morning."

"Morn-n-ing, Miss Agn-n…"

"…Mi-ss Agn-n-es."

They called all grown women "Miss", single women by their first name and married women by their surname.

Miss Agnes glanced up at the class through distracted eyes. Voice hoarse and wan, she said, "Siddown," having seated herself.

Once more the worm stirred inside Wheeler.

Wha she could do? She di' tell her is not her... She woulnt lissen!

Wheeler took her eyes away from Miss Agnes. She sat down and folded her arms on the desk.

Connected to each other, the dark wooden desks and matching benches sat low to the floor. The corner room was the weekday classroom for the school's youngest pupils. It was taken over now by thirty or so Sunday school children. An area of upturned chairs could be seen beyond the nursery doorway – open classes without walls – the lower elementary school, Donelle's weekday learning place.

Wheeler looked to where her cousin sat just beyond whispering distance on the other side of the U. Next to him sat the younger boy she had accused of starting the Christmas Sunday school pile-up. She had on more than one occasion told him he should tell Miss Agnes it had been him.

The register taken, pencil laid down, Miss Agnes looked at the faces in the room. "Who was John?" she enquired.

In their best clothes – colourful cotton dresses, crisp

buttoned shirts, a sunbeam every one – the room of shining faces turned glum: *Who was John?*

The teacher pointed to a boy on the left of the U. "Carl, go open d'side window." To another child she nodded. "Help him." Standing now at the front of the desk, Miss Agnes declared: "John has come."

Before the boy named Carl and the other child could return to the U, a contrary call and response began.

"*John has come.*"

"To testify."

"*T'testify.*"

"About d'coming of d'Lord."

"*Bout d'coming of d'Lord.*"

"Jesus will go into d'desert."

"*In d'desert.*"

"Will go *into* d'desert," Miss Agnes repeated.

"*In d'desert,*" the class repeated.

"To be tormented."

"*Be tormented.*"

"He will face torment for us."

"*Torment f'us.*"

"Christ will wander in d'desert."

"*D'desert.*"

"Will wander in d'desert for our sins."

"*Our sins.*"

"Christ will face torment an struggle."

"*An struggle.*"

"Christ will face *torment* and struggle!"

"Tormen' an struggle."

"In the bitter heat."

"Da bitter heat."

*"In d'*bitter heat!"

"Bitter heat!"

Miss Agnes's torment continued.

Wheeler's mind wandered. She started imagining Christ in the desert, unsure what a desert was. Instead she imagined Him setting off up the Cut, climbing all one hundred and sixty-three steps. Then in town, climbing Market Hill. She didn't have to try hard to conjure the bitter heat.

"John one, twenty-three. I am d'voice of one crying in d'wildaness."

"… In d'wildaness."

"Who was John?"

Wheeler blinked, realising Christ was no longer in the desert… realising she'd forgotten who John was.

W-ho was John? Wheeler glanced from left to right and left again.

"The voice of one crying in d'wild-a-ness!" Miss Agnes proclaimed.

"In da wil-da-ness."

"D'wil-da-ness," repeated Wheeler, latching onto the rambling sing-song.

Other distracted eyes were also trawling the room, including those of the small boy Wheeler had accused.

Sunday parting in his hair, sleepy eyes drifting, he looked little more than five years old. Donelle sat mumbling next to him. The younger boy looked as if a momentary lapse might send him slipping off the school bench to the floor.

Wheeler's frustration grew.

Wha she could do? He di' awready look like he warnt t'cry when she tell him.

"Make straight d'way o' d'Lord."

"*D'way o' d'Lord.*"

"I baptise wid water—"

Wha she could do? Miss Agnes woulnt lissen.

Wheeler's sense of injustice grew. She narrowed her eyes at Miss Agnes. Then, not wanting to, she looked again at the boy.

He little.

Wheeler turned away. She repeated the words the other children were saying, drifted along with them. Stared at a point at the front of the room. Once again, she sensed the unfairness of what had happened. But it had started to wane.

"Wha wrong wid you?"

Miss Bench!

After Sunday school, Wheeler stood waiting for her sisters to the side of the church entrance, away from the swirl of the congregation.

The large, perspiring features of Judith Bench lunged at

her. Wheeler's guilty heart thumped.

Wha wrong wid you—?

"Nutting wrong, Miss Bench." She cowered. "D'sun jus in meh eye."

Taller than any other woman in the churchyard, Miss Bench stooped closer to Wheeler, examined her: a specimen in a jar. "Y'learning yer lessons?"

"Yes, Miss Bench."

"Doing wha yer ant tell you?"

"Yes, Miss Bench."

Miss Bench didn't look so sure. She straightened up. "Whey y'sisters?"

"Dey jus talking to Miss Hughes, she talking t'dem." Wheeler pointed. To her surprise, when she turned round, Miss Bench was already on the move.

For a moment, Donelle came into view. Wheeler thought about them peeking into the Guide Hall—

Donelle ducked. He disappeared behind a curtain of people: men in felt hats, women in flowered dresses carrying their hymn books; everybody standing around talking at the same time in the cramped churchyard.

She in warnt nobody else t'see her.

Wheeler slipped out of sight against the church wall, behind the circling crowd. She tilted her eyes towards the steep retaining wall holding the schoolyard off the church. Enticing cries issued from above, where some children were still playing.

After Sunday school ended, Wheeler had run around the dirt-covered schoolyard, kicking up the dust, chasing other children with a new light-headedness. She hadn't seen the little boy again. Once the organ had stopped playing, once the church service was over, she'd looked for Donelle and Jonathan. All three had then raced for a distant flight of steps and descended into the narrow churchyard before it could become clogged. Now she, Donelle and Jonathan hung about waiting near the churchyard exit, hemmed in by the crowd.

Wheeler glared to where Adele and Hesta still stood talking to the young choirmistress.

How dey keep her waiting – why dey keep her waiting *for*?

Adele glanced round. She peeled away from the conversation.

"Y'going in d'choir?" Wheeler asked, her voice tetchy.

"Ah in tink so." Adele shook her head. "Ah hav enough t'do. Maybe Hesta," she suggested.

"B-but how she going in d'choir if we mudda sending f'us?" asked Wheeler.

Adele didn't respond. It wasn't clear whether or not she'd heard. She circled around, searching for the others. "Whey…?"

Jonathan stood near the exit to Churchway. From nowhere, with a sly look, Donelle crept forward into Adele's eyeview.

"Come on," Adele said.

"B-but we mudda sending f'us," Wheeler mumbled, following Adele.

Hesta stood to the side of the church door.

Eyes blazing, Wheeler criticised her: *She standing talking t'Miss Hughes, 'sif she going in d'choir.*

"Morning, Wheeler."

"Morning, Miss Hughes."

B-but...

Wheeler swivelled her head as she shuffled by.

But – *Hesta carnt sing!*

15

"When we mudda sending f'us?"

   "We in know. She only jus go. Giv her time."

   "B-but... when she sending f—"

   "Go t'sleep! We in know."

16

Lunchtime the following day. Having raced across Clarkton Road, Wheeler pursued Hesta. She elbowed her way through layers of children down the crowded elementary school steps. Donelle stood at the top of Churchway with a group of kids as she hurried by. Wheeler thought about waiting for him, but only for a moment.

He can follow when he warnt.

The midday sun found its way into the darkened alley, streaking the yellow bricks on the enclosing walls, highlighting Hesta as she passed the entrance to the churchyard. Sprinting down the alley, past the church, Wheeler turned onto Mill Street.

Mill Street ran glassy with heat. No cars in sight. A wave of white and grey and blue figures, disintegrating and quivering, spread across the road. Hesta moved among them. Wheeler set off towards Hesta, who was distinguishable by her height.

Glancing over her shoulder, Hesta gave Wheeler a dismissive look as she drew near. And Wheeler stared right back.

She in troubled bout Hesta trying t'lose her. She does always catch up.

A black dog lay curled up asleep between two houses on the right. Donelle came panting alongside, with another boy in tow. They trudged on, battling heat and sweat and the cruel light. Not a single shade tree in sight on the side of the road.

"Who can run faster – a mongoose or a iguana?" asked the boy.

A long moment passed.

Wheeler looked across at Donelle. He shook his head.

She di' see a mongoose whip up a tree on Cemet'ry Hill. She dint never see a iguana before.

"A mongoose," Wheeler said.

They took the drain alley down, as Hesta had done. There was no sign of Jonathan, who always made it back first for lunch. The riddling boy carried on along Mill Street on his own, not saying whether Wheeler was right or wrong.

On Russell Street the bay returned, the long aspect of it showing clear out to the port. There was a freighter moored at the harbour, at the end of the Longview. A red-and-black tug waited, moored outside the lumberyard, in the opening below.

At the junction with Cable Street, Hesta swirled around, fastening Donelle and Wheeler with a look, reminding them to stay off the road. Cars and motorbikes swooped up from the waterfront. Both children fumbled backwards to the roadside edge.

The day of the banana boat's return, Wheeler had stopped here at the Longview. She had stared at the ship's distant hull. She had started grieving and mumbling at the side of the road.

"D'ship di' come... from whey we mudda go. But we mudda in come back."

"Wha happ'ning?" Donelle had asked, panic in his voice, following her gaze off to the port.

It goan keep coming back.

Wheeler had remembered her aunt's simple words, had started walking alongside Donelle, having found the strength to head home.

Now a grey freighter stretched away in the distance. Hot seagulls wailed at the sky crying for their lunch. Wheeler walked alongside Donelle, not stopping at the Longview. Hesta pressed on ahead of them. As Hesta strobed through the broken shade at the back of the Cable & Wireless compound, Wheeler decided that her sister didn't care.

She in care we mudda gone. Dey in care like Tant'Celeste.

Their shadows touching, Donelle and Wheeler overtook Hesta at the bottom of the Cut, hurling their bird-light bodies at the punishing flights of little steps. Spots and panes of sunlight assailed them, pirouetting through the trees as they climbed, as Donelle and Wheeler raced one another.

High up, at the entrance to the family house, Wheeler broke away. Donelle came close behind, darting for the kitchen ramp. Wheeler slow-turned. Three neat plaits on her head, eyes full of envy, she watched as Donelle plunged his boy head under the water spilling from the tap.

17

Thursday morning on her way down the stairs, dressed in her school uniform, satchel slung to her back, Wheeler encountered Floyd on his way up. Donelle and Jonathan were scampering about in their room, maybe getting ready, maybe not. As she approached the middle step, Wheeler slowed down for Floyd to go past.

Floyd was wet from the shower. He had a bath towel around his waist and his eyes on her. She moved to get out of his way.

"Ah hear y'go in d'shop. Who sen y'in d'shop?" That look again, the one he'd given Wheeler the night he had stood over her on the kitchen stairs – less surprised, more curious this time.

Wheeler squinted.

He di' never question her before.

Gesturing with his head, Floyd said, "Who tell y'go down dere?"

Celeste stood in the well of the kitchen at the sink, her back to them. Wheeler's eyes darted down there. Then back.

"Y'in know who?"

Wheeler knew who. She dropped her eyes to the wooden stairs.

Was Celeste who sen people in d'shop – e'rybody know dat! He di' ask her sumting he awready know.

There was a look of puzzlement on Wheeler's face.

"W-ho?"

Reaching back for the satchel, Wheeler mumbled, "Tantie Celeste sen me."

"W-ho…?"

"Ah go f'Tant'Celeste."

A smile blossomed on Floyd's crooked lips. "'*Celeste sen me. Ah go f'Tant'Celeste*'," he mocked.

Wheeler appeared riled at hearing her words come out of his mouth.

"Y'tink people in see you?"

Who see her?

"Y'go f'Tantie Celeste?" There was pretend sympathy in Floyd's voice, faux empathy in the deep tilt of his head.

Wheeler looked to Celeste. Her aunt did not turn round.

Floyd said, "*Go* upstairs an say what y'do!"

Wha happ'ning? Wheeler asked herself.

Y'in trouble, came the answer.

Ah in warnt t'be in trouble. Ah in warnt t'go upstairs.

Y'in trouble—

Ah in warnt t'go upstairs by Tant'Innez. Ah in warnt anudda lash!

The left side of Wheeler's leg tingled. The competing voices played on all the way up the stairs. She jolted. Floyd was following her.

He coming right behind—

Y'better hurry up den!

Wheeler hurried. As she tapped on his mother's bedroom door, Floyd brushed past, not bothering with her.

"Ur-gh?"

On hearing her aunt grunt, Wheeler nudged at the part-open door and crept into Innez's bedroom. There was a large brass bed to the left of the door. Innez sat perched on the bed, back turned, pinning up her hair.

Wheeler fumbled and stared, waiting until spoken to.

The folds of Innez's neck rolled open with every tilt of her head. Her plump hands weaved then pinned up her plaits.

Plump hands f'giving two lash! Wheeler looked away.

The view from the tall windows was of the vast sky, the headland and the fort high on the edge of the promontory.

A line of ironed clothes hung in the corner of the room, among them crisp white tunics, Innez's work clothes. Innez worked in the government dispensary in town.

"H-gh." Grunting and sighing, she finished off plaiting. Innez inched round. The moment had arrived.

Wheeler's account came out all at once: "Ah - ah go on d'Wharf t'buy d'bread f'Tant'Celeste an Floyd say ah hav t'come up here."

"Wha y'say!" Innez spluttered, spidery hairpins in her mouth.

Recoiling hard against the bedroom wall, Wheeler started again. "Ah di' go on d'Wharf. To buy some bread f'Tant'Celeste. An… an Floyd say ah hav t'come up here."

Y'wha? Who? Innez's sour features seemed to say. "Y'know you shoulnt go down dere? Y'could *drung* yerself!" The eyeglasses jumped as she spoke.

"Ah in know dat." The signalling light of the bread shop twinkled in Wheeler's mind.

"Y'in know dat *who*?"

"Ah in know dat… Tantie Innez."

Innez's myopic gaze lingered on Wheeler.

Wheeler's scrawny legs trembled in anticipation of what was to come. The cloth satchel slipped to her side. She grabbed hold of the strap.

Innez spoke. "Clean out d'sitting room cabinet when y'get home. Look at me! Polish d'ornaments, y'hear?"

"Yes, Tantie Inn-e-z—"

"Every last one o' dem. *Polish* dem! Til y'see yer black face in dem."

"Yes, Tantie Innez."

"*Go!*"

Outside the door, Wheeler's eyes focused on Floyd's bedroom. She paused, attempting to figure something out.

Who say dey see her? She dint let nobody see her!

At the top of the stairs, she ran through the journey to the bread shop in her head.

She di' see udda people relative walking home. Did remember t'not look at dem: dey carnt see her if she in see dem. Who di' see her?

On her way down the stairs, expecting to find Celeste, Wheeler instead heard the shuffle of someone getting away. She called out: "Tant'Celeste!"

The sound of vanishing continued under the stairs, round to her aunt's bedroom.

"Tantie Ce-lest-e?" Wheeler cried, but Celeste did not come out.

"Wha wrong wid *you*?"

By the time Adele came down, Wheeler was standing beside the concrete sink. Eyes deadened, she turned her whole body towards the sound of her sister's voice.

Not waiting on an answer, Adele shoved a stack of schoolbooks into Wheeler's chest. Wheeler's short arms embraced them on a reflex. Adele hurried back into the house.

Wha wrong?

Wheeler's eyes fell on the open field of water.

It *all* di' go wrong!

"Awright." Adele returned and snatched her books.

Wheeler followed her: down the ramp, over the packed earth at the front of the house, her legs running ahead while her mind stood still. She came to a halt under Celeste's bedroom.

It all di' go wrong.

"Wha y'doing? Come on. *Come!*"

Wheeler's legs faltered at the start of the tumbling steps.

She di' go in d'shop f'Tantie Celeste. Now she get in trouble, Tant'Celeste di' leave her all by sheself.

Coming back home for lunch, walking down Churchway, she told Donelle about her punishment, told him about what she'd done. To her confusion Donelle reacted as if *he'd* done something wrong.

"Why y'go down dere?"

Wheeler was unprepared for this.

"Y'shoulnta go down dere."

Wheeler's lips fell open, her eyes bulged.

Wha... why he telling her bout dat fa? She in warnt t'hear how she coulda drung sheself. Again.

Something occurred to Wheeler. She fixed her face. She sweetened her reaction. "Why y'in help me when school done... help me polish dem?"

Donelle turned away a little, as if distancing himself from her and her problem. "Ah playing wid Christopher an dem."

This astonished Wheeler. "Wh-h... Christopher an he brudda!" She came to a halt. Considered Donelle with scorn.

Bwoys he di' play wid fore she come an live on d'hill. Bwoys e'rybody know was jus babies.

Donelle kept his distance.

Wheeler said, "You… we can go down by Christopher an dem after."

Donelle kept his eye glued to the shiny, hot surface of Mill Street, as he got further away.

Wheeler ran to catch up with him. Pulled his arm.

Donelle swung round at her. "Wha if sumting break? Wha go happen den?" he said, almost tearful.

"We wont break nutting—"

"How y'know we wont break nutting?"

"How we go break sumting?"

Other children filed past. The cousins stood arguing at the side of the road.

"Ah di' stay an help if it was you," Wheeler said.

Donelle scrutinised her, seeming unsure.

Wheeler stood in front of Donelle with wide scheming eyes, one hair ribbon undone. "Y'jus fraid f'yerself!" she taunted.

Donelle walked off, blending in with the hazy lunchtime crowd on Mill Street.

Wheeler gaped after him. Blasted by the midday sun, she lowered her gaze. She stared at her hapless shadow. "M'head hutting me!" she told it.

The old display cabinet contained large and small ornaments, Regency figurines, Bo-Peep and her sheep, tiny commemorative spoons as well as numerous pieces of crockery and glassware.

How she goan polish dem! She in self tink she an Donelle could finish dem. How… how she goan finish by sheself?

Though it had been four weeks since the errand to the shop, Wheeler had told no one about it. Not Adele on the way to school. Not Hesta – not that she'd tell Hesta, who appeared now in the distance, or someone looking like Hesta, across the bending, jumping heat. She knew what her sisters would have said: Y'tink we mudda leave so y'could get yerself in some commesse bout going in d'shop?

"Is not m'fault!" Wheeler contended, running now to catch up as the Hesta-like girl faded away.

By the time Wheeler emerged on Russell Street, Donelle had already stretched several feet ahead.

She in self tell him wha he brudda di' say.

Her eyes grew cloudy.

Asking who sen her in d'shop, when he done know awready.

Tink people in see you? Go upstairs an say wha y'do!

Leaving Russell Street, the gap between Donelle and Wheeler grew smaller. In spite of herself, she thought about what he'd said. She imagined something from the cabinet falling, breaking.

Donelle glanced back and stopped climbing. He let her catch up to him.

As they arrived at the long, level landing, the noise of a short-wave radio greeted them from one of the wooden houses: helicopter gunships, the roar of their propellers ricocheting and echoing around the slope. Amid the ammunition, the blur of words they had heard before – Vietcong, Ho Chi Minh City, Saigon.

"At least y'dint get licks," Donelle told her in between the noise of the overseas news.

Wheeler winced, thinking of what lay ahead.

No, he mudda in giv her licks. Not yet.

Later that afternoon, changed out of her school clothes, Wheeler lurked in the shade at the back of the house. From there she followed the comings and goings of the others: Jonathan leaving from the veranda entrance; Donelle setting out soon afterwards, off to play with Christopher and his brother; Adele climbing the ramp and heading into the kitchen. Wheeler lay low so no one would see her.

Hearing her sisters chatting in the bedroom above, she crouched under the side window where she waited for the room to go quiet, for her sisters to head up to the Girl Guide meeting. Unable to see the Cut, there was a tense pause as Wheeler tried to determine whether the time had come for her to step out from the side of the house and make her way to the sitting room.

As she entered the sitting room, her features soured at the sight of Hesta.

Wha she doing? She sister inside d'cabinet – not in Guides, not in she uniform!

Kneeling in front of the display cabinet, Hesta's exposed heels pointed out behind her into the room. The long, glass doors were flung open to either side of her.

'Sif…

Wheeler flinched, putting together what she was seeing.

Hesta. D'cabinet. 'Sif she awready *know*!… Adele could be nice, but Hesta di' always warnt her t'be in trouble.

Wheeler turned to run.

"Stay whey y'deh!" Hesta yelled, twisting on all fours. "Wha it is y'do?"

"Ah in do nut-ting."

"Ah taut we tell y't'stay outa trouble?"

"Ah in do nutt—!"

"Hush! Ah goan find out anyhow."

Though she remained where she was, Wheeler was still aching to run. "Why y'not in Guides?"

Hesta gave her an ugly look. "How ah can go in Guides? Celeste say ah hav t'help you."

"Whey Adele?"

Hesta didn't answer that. "Come." She invited Wheeler into the room.

Still in the doorway, Wheeler took the measure of her sister: her tightened lips, the cutting look.

She dint like being alone wid Hesta.

The sitting room was to the right of the doorway. There

was a circle of mahogany armchairs near the middle windows, and a side table under the far window festooned in crocheted doilies and ornaments that Wheeler hadn't been instructed to shine. A blonde-faced radiogram stared from beside the display cabinet, dark round dials for eyes. Both radiogram and cabinet stood with their backs against the wall adjoining Innez's bedroom. The large, three-sided room had a formal, silent quality about it. Its open side looked across at Floyd's and the younger brothers' bedrooms.

Wheeler walked further in.

Most of the room's contents had belonged to her grandparents or other longer-dead relatives. Innez would sometimes eat her meals seated at the low table on the far side of the room. Now and then Floyd would stroll in to turn on the goggle-eyed radiogram for the midday news.

Seated on the floor, Wheeler's eyes glanced from one solemn piece of dark wood furniture to another. The room was the only place she could remember having seen her mother in this house: the night of her departure, standing facing Innez.

Wheeler glanced down. On the bare wooden floor were large figurines, which Hesta had laid out ahead of Wheeler's arrival. Hesta laid out a handful more. "Shine dem. Take dat dusting cloth" – she pointed – "an rub dem down. Ah goan put out some more." Legs folded under her, Hesta launched into the upright cabinet and then shuffled backwards. She deposited more objects around her little sister, seated head down, dust cloth in hand.

Wheeler tensed up. She sensed her sister's smooth, accusing eyes press into her. She grabbed hold of the nearest object and started shining, small hands churning.

The display cabinet was of a kind to be found in most homes on the island. Made of mahogany or a lesser painted wood, the cabinets were filled with unusable items.

Their mother's display cabinet had hung against the kitchen wall. Instead of glass, there was fine metal mesh on its double doors. Seeing that other cabinet in her mind's eye, Wheeler lifted her head.

When a big truck di' pass d'house, spoons an cups an tings did tinkle.

A jumping, merry sound that Wheeler heard now.

That cabinet was painted the generous, creamy yellow of the sun following a bout of rain. One day, neighbours had started taking the cabinet items away, collecting things her mother had promised to them for helping her out. The sunny yellow cabinet had sold for a few dollars, contributing to her mother's boat fare.

D'shiny plates an spoons an everyting di' go. Dey in hav nutting f'deyself—

Wheeler knelt up. After finishing each dusted item, she reached out and placed it away from the rest. From the corner of her eye, she spied on her sister. Hesta cradled some of the smaller ornaments in her arms. She squeaked over to

Wheeler, shuffling back and forth on her bended legs. The room smelled of floor wax and warm dust, of the vinegar water they would use to clean the cabinet glass. Wheeler's young fingers turned and dusted and shined, twitched like the legs of a grappling baby crab. Hesta shuffled back.

The big-eyed radiogram regarded them in the waxy silence as they worked. After a while Wheeler cried out, "Why ah hav t'polish all o' dem?"

A harrowing moment followed as both she and Hesta froze.

Innez's bedroom was on the other side of the sitting room wall. Floyd's bedroom was across the way to her left. Wheeler twisted her head towards the part-open door. What could Floyd do? In all her time in the house, he'd never paid her any mind. More than once, he'd reached past her to give Donelle a lash. She had seen him box Jonathan in his mouth and then stroll past her as if she hadn't been standing right there watching. But now…

"Y'ain in enough trouble yet?" asked Hesta.

Wheeler's eyes remained fixed on Floyd's bedroom door. "Ah di' go by d'Wharf f'Tant'Celeste, an he find out."

Hesta sneered as if to say, Ah did tell you ah goan find out. "Y'tink we mudda working she arse off in Ingland so you can get yerself in trouble whey y'deh?"

No. Wheeler didn't think that.

"Well, he ain in dere now," Hesta said. "Here."

A painful look came into Wheeler's eyes as she turned round. Alongside all the little objects already on the floor, Hesta had left a jumble of yellowed shot glasses for her to dust and shine.

A small red light shone in the distance above the fort. Blurry darkness marked out the fortifications below. There were colourful lights elsewhere on the headland. Hovering at Innez's bedroom doorway, Wheeler stared, before slinking in.

"Y'polish d'ornaments?"

"Yes, Tant'Innez."

"Y'break anyting?"

"No, Tant'Innez."

Descending the kitchen stairs, Wheeler took a new look at the scene below: Adele standing in the middle of the kitchen, pointing, nodding, in discussion with Celeste; Donelle waiting for his supper in his place at the turn of the stairs; and Floyd at the counter, half-seated on a stool near the bottom step.

Wha could Floyd do?

She sat down.

The bare light bulb to her left sent its feeble light around the kitchen reaching as far as it could; the tall, unpainted walls receded in darkness where it could not.

He mudda dint hit her dis time. Jus tell her go downstairs f'she food.

Wheeler's eyes rested on Floyd, tilted and rocking on the wooden stool.

"Whey y'bin?" Donelle asked in a hoarse whisper from the middle of the stairs.

Wheeler and Hesta had managed to do what Wheeler had been tasked to do. They had emptied the display cabinet, dusted and shined its contents. Before returning the items, Hesta had cleaned and shined the cabinet's glass doors. Far from taking the lifetime Wheeler had feared, they had finished in good time for supper.

Donelle's eyes were on her. Now her punishment was done, Wheeler told herself she could just ignore him.

Is he own biznis if he warnta go by Carter Hill an play wid Christopher an dem.

Looking around, Wheeler realised there was something she was aware of, other than Donelle annoying her. Something unsaid tucked underneath the usual cries of the crickets coming in from the yard.

Adele and Celeste drew apart, bringing their discussion to a close. "Awright, we ready!" yelled Celeste.

Wheeler waited before going down, pressing her head against the stair posts. She watched the activity unleashed by Celeste's shout. Both Jonathan and Hesta came in from the night. They took a cup of cocoa tea each and a plate. Adele did the same. Her sisters and Jonathan went out into the yard.

Donelle came struggling up the stairs with his mother's

cup and plate. Everything in the kitchen, everyone was as she'd seen them before. Nothing new. Except...

Wheeler tipped forward.

E'rybody di' keeping outa Floyd way, one way or udda. E'rybody di' minding deyself – wid Floyd sitting dere.

18

The following morning, Wheeler went down to be with Celeste.

The kitchen presented its usual morning face: a layer of soft shadow on the L-shaped counter, a grey square of light at the metal sink. On the bottom corner of the house, west-facing, it wouldn't be much brighter at midday than it was now.

Wheeler jumped into the well of the kitchen, righted herself and headed for the lavatory on the passage under the stairs. Having relieved herself, she stood in her flimsy nightdress staring out through the kitchen doorway.

Celeste was bent double, rummaging out in the bushes by the chicken coop. Seagulls shrieked across the grey neck of the bay. The arm of the Anglican clock pointed to ten past six. An angry hen flew up at Celeste as she reversed back from the bushes and she flung the Rhode Island Red to the ground with a rapid swipe of her arm.

Wheeler pulled back. "M-orning."

Celeste kept her eyes on the pecking hens. She hugged the feed bucket against her hip, saying nothing. As she approached the doorway, Wheeler stepped aside. Then followed her in.

Celeste took the eggs from the bucket and started washing them under the tap.

Dragging over a wobbling stool and kneeling up on it, Wheeler positioned herself near to her aunt. She reached across the deep counter and pulled over the basin and swizzle stick, ready to mix. Wheeler watched as Celeste began cracking the eggs – whites and yolks – into the enamel basin. *Ne'er mind wha di' happen,* Wheeler told herself. *Tant'Celeste dint stop her from getting in trouble, but she di' sen Hesta t'help.*

"Ah shine d'ornament. Wid Hesta," Wheeler said, studying the side of Celeste's long, clasped face. She just wanted the closeness to her aunt to return.

The silence continued.

Someone had started blowing a lambie conch. The sound of it was throaty and curved. Celeste lifted her eyes. "Go on upstairs. Get yer sisters out o' bed. Don't pass yer time no more in dis kitchen—"

"But ah—"

"*Go.*"

Wheeler gazed into Celeste's face. The hardened jaw, the cruel eyes. The look on her aunt's face was overpowering.

She di' see she ant look vex, she di' see her look tired an fed up. She in never see her look dat way before.

Celeste took the swizzle stick out of Wheeler's hand—

There was no resistance from Wheeler.

Then Celeste flattened the swizzle stick between her own ragged palms and started mixing the eggs.

Seizing the edge of the countertop for support, Wheeler struggled off the trembling stool. She did not know *when* her feet touched the floor. She regarded her aunt with wonder – the alien arc of her neck, the scatter of little plaits – and backed away.

"Wha happen t'you? How y'in downstairs wid Celeste?"

Adele's heckling tone brought Wheeler crashing back to herself. She stared up at her sister, slipped past and lowered herself onto the bed. She didn't want to talk to Adele or Hesta – not to anyone who'd tried to warn her to leave Celeste alone.

"Celeste in y'mudda," said Hesta, laying out their school clothes on the bed.

Wheeler kept her eyes on the clothes.

"Come an ah plait y'hair. Y'can go in d'shower when Hesta come back."

Eyes lowered, Wheeler went and sat on the floor in front of Adele.

She di' lose fren wid Tant'Celeste. She di' come used t'helping she ant. Tant'Celeste di' show her how t'do d'eggs, d'orange peel t'put in d'pot… She dint know if she could face she ant again—

"Ow!"

"Sorry. Bend yer head."

Adele loosened the last of the plaits at the back of Wheeler's head and started combing out her hair.

Eyes down, body trapped between Adele's smooth brown legs, something tugged at Wheeler's mind.

Floyd di' get her in trouble, he di' get her in trouble.

The stray gaggle from a chicken toddling in the bushes. In the room, there was the glistening smell from the Vaseline Adele was using on Wheeler's hair. Her eyes widened as she thought about what Floyd had done.

Floyd di' make her say *who*. Tant'Celeste di' go in she room.

Finished plaiting Wheeler's hair, Adele stood up and patted her on the shoulder, urging her to get up. A dead housefly dangled near their schoolbooks, caught in an invisible web. Wheeler remained cross-legged on the floor, staring at the corner of the room.

"How come Floyd in like Tant'Celeste?"

Adele appeared to lose her stride. Other children sailed past them on the way to school.

"Floyd in like nobody," said Adele, recovering. She picked up the pace.

Wheeler hopped after her to keep up.

Who tell y'go down dere?

"How come he trowing words f'Tant'Celeste?"

Adele took her time before answering. She had a pinched

112

look on her face. "Dat's jus how he does kerry on," she said. "Don't trouble yerself." Pressing down on Wheeler's shoulder, she brought her to a halt and then steered her across the road towards the houseshop.

Wheeler had braced herself coming back from the shower, afraid of bumping into Celeste. She had looked all around, had managed to get back up to the bedroom without seeing her aunt. When Wheeler collected her breakfast plate, it was just Hesta in the kitchen doling out the brown cocoa tea. It was only on leaving the house that Wheeler had seen her aunt, hanging washing at the top of the yard.

"Tant'Celeste, we going!" And again, "We going," Adele had cried out.

"Urr-*hm*," Celeste had answered, but she did not look round.

Outside the houseshop, Wheeler frowned. "W-wha if he hit me – like he does hit Jonaton an Donelle?"

Adele sighed. "He carnt hit you. Y'mudda in leave you wid Floyd. She leave you wid Innez. Stay here." Adele went into the shop.

The roadside shop took up the ground floor of a two-storey house. A pile of breeze blocks served to hold the front door wide open. A line of children stretched from the doorway to the counter, while others headed back out the other way.

A boy Wheeler knew came struggling around the outside of the house hefting a kerosene can. Climbing from the sidewalk to join him, she said, "Linky, y'in going t'school?" He was dressed in the same grey shortpants and white cotton shirt worn by Jonathan and Donelle.

"Yeh, ah going."

Soft-spoken, not much taller than Wheeler, the boy guided the square can away from her legs. The box-can gurgled and kicked as though there were something living in it.

"Y'not goan be late?"

Prob'ly, Linky's faint smile seemed to say.

As Wheeler spoke, both glanced towards a blue-gabled bungalow across the road from the Cable & Wireless. Linky's destination. He undertook chores for the two old sisters who lived in the house, ran errands for them before and after school. His mother received one red dollar bill at the end of each month in return.

The kerosene can collided with Linky's chalky legs.

"Y'in coming an play dis Saturday?"

He lowered his eyes and shook his head. "Ah hav t'help out," he said, walking away.

Adele came from the shop carrying a paper bag, the word *Modess* visible inside the thin brown bag. "Come, na." She twisted Wheeler round as the boy headed the other way.

19

Over the coming days, the heat of the day expanded, the brightness of the sea became hard-edged. White light bounced and flickered with the roll of the waves. Sweat gathered in the folds of Wheeler's neck from early on and trickled down her sides from the small cups of her underarms. School grew harder in the suffering heat. She was forgetting things she already knew.

Called to the teacher's desk in the small passageway of the school, Wheeler stared mesmerised as the teacher pointed to a place inside an exercise book. Leaning from her toes to the height of the tall wooden desk, Wheeler tipped her nose into the book.

"Wha happ'ning dere?" the teacher asked.

Wheeler eyeballed the lengthy hopscotch of long division: piles and blocks and stacks of her own work grown unrecognisable in the heat.

The teacher lifted the book away from Wheeler's nose. "Y'in know yer tables?… Y'not going t'secondary school?"

Eyes lingering on the upheld exercise book, Wheeler

lowered herself to the floor. "But ah not going t'secondry scho-o—"

"Chil'ren in Ingland know all dey times tables. Go. Write out y'eight times table."

Wheeler retrieved her book.

The heat intensified as the days dragged on.

Afternoons, Wheeler and Donelle found themselves drawn to the shade of the massive poui trees north of the Guide Hall wall, the exposed rootbed like a risen underground map. They pitted themselves against the roots, seeking pockets of comfort in the thin afternoon shade. No hint of cooling even as the soft, black nights drew near.

One sweltering morning, before the hot spell ended, Wheeler's mind returned to something more discomforting than the heat.

Who tell Floyd dey see her when she go in d'bread shop? Floyd ain in d'band practice. He di' come back from work late. She di' see people wining t'd'band. She di' cross d'gap *way* t'd'side.

Y'tink people in see you?

She dint tink nobody see her! When dey see her? When she going or when she come out?

Wheeler's thoughts jostled with one another as she and Adele hurried to school. A woman appeared from the side of a house.

"Morning," said Adele.

"All-you awright?" the woman answered.

Wheeler regarded the woman with quick suspicion.

Dere was always people seeing dem, knowing who dey belong to. Dey does know who y'belong to, even if y'in know dem.

The week before, a white-haired woman had come out of the houseshop, had accosted Wheeler and Donelle: "*Wha* all-you doing?"

Dey in doing nutting. Dey jus warnt t'see wha udda people di' see.

Older children had been running back up Russell Street. One said, "All-you come, he peeing in d'drain. Come see!"

"Go home," the old woman had said. "In *nutting* f'all y't'see. All-you ant waiting home f'all-you!"

Wheeler and Donelle had gaped at one another. *Dey in know d'woman!*

They'd missed what the other children had seen.

"Why all-you standing up in d'street, watching udda chil'ren act d'fool?"

Celeste had already known what had happened before they got home.

Adele hurried Wheeler past the Russell Street gap. The seafront was lit up. Sunlight poured over the rum shop steps. Wheeler slowed down a little. She realised she might never know *who* had told Floyd they'd seen her.

The night of the bread shop there'd been a man seated on the shallow steps leading to the rum shop porch as

Wheeler stared out to the shore. There'd been two other men hunched over the top railing by the door.

Wheeler had glanced at the men and then looked away.

"Ain let nobody see you," Celeste had said. She didn't think she meant them.

20

One day after school, Wheeler waited at the side of Clarkton Road. End of day noises trickled like water from the elementary school forecourt into Churchway. A final noisy group of children approached the police signal box. The rowdy sounds of pupils making their way home continued to dwindle in every direction.

Whey Hesta?

Waiting for her sister, the look of expectation on Wheeler's face changed to worry. She wondered what was going on.

The only sound left was of a group of teenagers seated on the school steps talking with their backs to the road. One of them turned. "Y'looking f'yer sister?"

Wheeler nodded.

The girl with a kind voice and twists in her hair stood up and came to the kerb. After checking for a gap in the traffic, she stepped into the road. She held out her hand. Wheeler met her halfway, surprised by this approach.

Was Hesta job t'take her home. How she could leave her an go!

"Y'sister in gone yet," called the girl.

Part way to the alleyway, Wheeler glanced back.

"She still upstairs."

Wheeler stopped.

E'rybody else di' gone, 'cluding Jonaton an Donelle. Why she sister upstairs... how she in gone?

The teenagers started dispersing: some headed for Churchway, others strode up Clarkton Road, including the girl with the twists. Their leaving filled Wheeler's ears as she approached the silent school entrance. She reached for the iron handrail. At the top of the stairs, she peered in around the open doorway. A graveyard of upturned chairs stretched to the far side of the school. At the distant sound of a scraping chair she fled into the enclosed staircase.

A storm of dust motes raged in the overhead light. Wheeler hesitated then crept up the soft wooden steps, perspiration breaking out on her face. There was the sense of an unquiet, peopled silence as she climbed to the top of the stairs.

"Who you?"

Who? Wheeler wobbled. She was lucky not to have tipped backwards.

At the sound of the man's voice, a number of gaping faces swung round to look at her – Hesta's was one of them. "She m'sister, sir," she said, raising her hand.

Laying down his pen, the teacher eased onto his feet

at the head of the captive group. He looked directly at Wheeler. "Yer sister in detention. *Get* out!" he said.

Wheeler rattled down the stairs and out of the building. Still running, she grabbed hold of the iron handrail.

Who him?

She clambered up to the cobbled shade where the teenagers had been, swung around and sat down. Her chest tightened. Her mind clattered through what had happened.

She di' nearly drop down! D'teacher di' see her— all o' dem di' see her. He di' nearly make her fall down.

Yet all of it counted for nothing against what she'd learnt: *Yer sister in detention.*

Wheeler's mood brightened. How she sister in detention – when Hesta di' all d'time saying *she* should stay outa trouble?

She looked up. Her eyes scaled the height of the stone-clad building where Hesta was. Then dropped to the ground floor entrance. Two teenage girls were tumbling out of the school, tugging and pulling one another. Raising a finger to her lips, the smaller one grabbed hold of the other, eyes tilted to the top windows. Wheeler watched them dart across the school forecourt, heard their muffled snorts as they raced down Churchway. She peered as they disappeared around the churchyard entrance.

From over on Church Street the Anglican church bell sent out its dull, hard *clack*, making her jump.

Quarter past four. School finished at half three.

When dey go get home? Wha Tant'Celeste goan say? Wha if she ask whey dey bin?

Wheeler's eyes returned to the school's upper floor.

By the time Hesta came out, there was a man and a woman teacher standing talking in the school entrance. They looked her sister up and down. Wheeler leaned forward.

A new exchange started taking place, a tense one, with the teachers' eyes on Hesta. Hesta dipped her head.

From the far reaches of the Clarkton Road steps Wheeler looked on, satisfied. Unable to hear, she could nevertheless imagine what was being said: Dey telling she sister bout she behaviour. Bout how she *wasting* people time getting sheself in detention. All d'same ting Hesta woulda tell her – if *she* be d'one in trouble.

After a long while with Hesta standing between them, with neither of the teachers speaking, one of them pivoted out of the way. Hesta walked down from the entrance and Wheeler stood up off the steps.

Making her way across the opening, Hesta said, "C'mon," and cast an irritated glance at Wheeler.

A spark of outrage in Wheeler's eyes, as she bounced down towards her sister.

She in d'one in trouble!

Then she remembered the question Hesta had asked *her* when they were polishing the ornaments: *"Wha it is y'do?"*

Dropping back, narrowing her eyes, Wheeler mumbled the words again and again: "Wha it is y'do?"

Two darkened figures flew out from the churchyard, an air of frenzy about them. A haphazard descent then followed, all three girls guffawing as they fell towards the street below.

"Wha he say?"

"Wha he could say?"

Their voices echoed inside the long, dark cave of the alleyway.

Landing on Mill Street, howling, the trio stopped joking around and started sharing something round. A look of realisation came into Wheeler's face.

A ray of sunlight fell across the surface of the road. The two friends disappeared out of the light, off towards King Street, where the traffic box was. Hesta strolled off the other way.

Wheeler followed her sister along Mill Street, now blessed by afternoon shade. The day had passed its boiling point. Wheeler's resentment flared.

All d'time... all d'time Hesta di' make her tink *she* was d'one making trouble. But it was Hesta. Hesta d'one all d'time causing trouble sheself!

Past the cover of the church building, Hesta walked on. Approaching a row of bungalows, she slowed down and looked back, long arms cradling her schoolbooks.

Hesta's a *teef*! Wheeler concluded. Even if she di' fast

sometimes t'mind udda people biznis, least she in never *teef* nutting.

Hand on hip, Hesta called back to her: "Wha y'doing?"

Wheeler took her time.

A jerry-rigged shelf extended from one of the bungalow windows, creating a shadow on the shoulderless road. A selection of homemade treats sat bunched in small bundles on the window shelf. Hesta stood in front of them. Wheeler approached.

A crowd of people were singing on the radio – "*We shall overco-o-ome*" – voices crackling and wavering, a wrenching sound which Wheeler had heard before.

Her fraught eyes tightened. She peered through the dark bungalow. She could make out nothing but the strait of blue water in the back window.

"Afternoon, Miss Tiny," Hesta said, bent over at the window shelf.

A woman came, slow-footed, into view as Wheeler's eyes grew accustomed to the gloom.

"Afternoon," said Wheeler. The crowd kept on singing from overseas. A different overseas from where her mother was.

From whey war di' always happ'ning. Whey people di' always singing...

"*We shall overcome, so-o-me da-y…*" Wheeler squinted, half-listening.

"Wha y'like?" The old woman smiled, her face a mass

gathering of tiny moles.

Wheeler's eyes rifled through what had been left unbought by other children who had already made their way home. Tamarind balls. Red and brown boiled sweets on sticks – Red Boys and N-Boys. Groundnut sugar cakes. Paltry offerings, yet still beyond Hesta's and Wheeler's means. Neither one ever had any money.

"Ah go hav a N-Boy please, Miss Tiny," declared Hesta, then added, "Wha y'like?" glancing down at Wheeler.

Wheeler's accusing gaze remained glued to Hesta's face.

Reaching out, Hesta took the N-Boy from Miss Tiny in one hand. Wheeler's eyes twinkled at the miracle of the silver coin in her sister's other hand.

Paying her grim little sister no mind, Hesta strolled away, sucking the hard boiled sweet, rolling it around her tongue, shoving it back and forth between her lips.

She had t'tell somebody. Hesta's a *teef!*

They had returned home later than usual. As they drifted in, Celeste had just looked up and glanced at them. Wheeler need not have worried. Their aunt had not spoken, as if not caring *where* they'd been.

She had t'tell Adele so she sister could *know*. Hesta in d'way she does preten'.

After supper, Adele stood alone in the kitchen, scraping the frying pan at the metal sink.

Going down into the kitchen, Wheeler was wrong-footed.

"Wha all-you saying?" asked Adele.

Jonathan rolled in from the darkness in the yard – and then Hesta.

Wheeler retreated up the stairs.

Later, as Wheeler got ready for bed, her sisters came into the bedroom *together*.

The following morning, Wheeler stuck close to Adele on the rickety journey down to school, informing on Hesta still uppermost in her mind.

Every little *ting* Hesta does tell bout her! Does act 'sif she in never do nutting wrong!

Anticipation welled up inside Wheeler. She hurried after Adele at the bottom of the Cut.

She hav t'tell. Bout dem gyuls waiting round f'Hesta. Tell bout d'teacher. So Adele *know* wha Hesta do.

Instead, as Wheeler caught up to her, it was Adele who spoke first. She asked, "Wha it is y'tink Hesta do?"

Wheeler's foot misstepped.

Adele *know*? B…bu-t.

"How y'mean?" Confusion and wonder combined in Wheeler's voice.

How she could know?

The night before, Hesta had behaved as though nothing notable had happened. Had treated her younger sister with no less ill grace than usual. Had collected her supper plate alongside Wheeler, ignoring her.

Looking sideways at Wheeler, Adele let out a heavy sigh. "Wha if it not her? Wha if she in *teef* nutting?"

Wheeler's mouth sagged open.

Adele scrutinised her. "Y'in tell Donelle?"

Wheeler shook her head.

Adele walked on. Wheeler followed.

A small brown bird hopscotched in the shade ahead. It hopped in line with the schoolchildren marching along the road. Brows pinched, Wheeler gazed at the bird.

B-but she di' *know* tings bout Hesta. She di' *hear* wha Adele di' saying. B-ut d'both o' dem carnt be true.

The world had made more sense to Wheeler moments before, when Hesta was a thief.

"Wha if she jus see dem take it?" Adele suggested. "Y'warnt yer sister t'be in trouble?"

The small bird flew away.

The question hung unanswered in the air.

21

Maybe she *should* get in trouble?

Saturday morning, sweeping the terraced yard, Wheeler wiggled her waist from side to side, to the rhythm of the list inside her head:

Styling her off.

Telling her t'*mind she own biznis.*

An keep outa trouble.

Wheeler slowed down wiggling.

So wha if Hesta di' help her out *once*? She still in d'person she does preten'. Telling her not t'do tings when she doing tings sheself!

Before walking away to the convent school, Adele had once again asked Wheeler, "Wha it is y'tink Hesta do?"

Eyes landing on Adele's prefect badge, Wheeler had frowned. She no longer knew what she wanted to be true. Now, as she hugged the yard broom, her mind returned to Adele: *Dere was d'truth, den dere was wha people does say – quick an easy jus like dat!*

"Meh church shoe squeezing me. When we mudda goan send d'money?"

She remembered what had happened when she and Adele went to town to buy a new pair of shoes.

Turning onto George Street, all of a sudden Adele had warned Wheeler to start behaving herself. "An stand up straight."

"How ah not behaving meself? Why ah mus…"

A glimmer of understanding had registered on Wheeler's face. Someone was headed their way. Transported on the gentle tide of people doing their Saturday shopping, there was no mistaking who that someone was. Face bright and sour like an orange, Miss Ogilvy had Adele and Wheeler in her sights.

Adaila Ogilvy had been their mother's schoolteacher. She blocked their way. "Wha all-you doing in town?"

"Morning, Miss Ogilvy."

Ignoring Wheeler, Miss Ogilvy asked the question again – of Adele: "Wha y'doing in town?"

Adele hesitated, not answering. To Wheeler's astonishment. Wheeler squeezed hold of Adele's hand. She squeezed it again. No response.

Grown women had questioned Wheeler all her life – in the churchyard, on the way to school, on the street walking home.

Y'hav t'tell dem wha dey warnt!

On the verge of saying just *that*, she'd peeked at Adele out of the corner of her eye.

In the end Adele had responded to Miss Ogilvy, had released Wheeler's hand. "Good morning, Miss Ogilvy."

"How come," Miss Ogilvy wanted to know, "every time ah see you dese days, y'strolling round town? Is big 'oman y'turn now?"

"Ah taking Wheeler t'buy she new church shoes," Adele answered.

Miss Ogilvy held Adele's gaze. "And wha you doing in town last week Wensday?"

"Ah come on a errand. Wheeler writing slate break. Ah hav t'buy her a new one."

And dat's how lying does go, Wheeler recalled. Quick an easy jus like dat. A new writing slate she in never get!

"Ne'er mind Miss Ogilvy," she sister di' say. "She like mindin' people biznis too much."

Wheeler swung round dragging the broom.

There was a row going on. Raised voices were coming from the other side of the house. Wheeler looked towards the top windows.

Harsh urgent sounds were spilling out of Innez's bedroom. "Y'in hear ah talking? Ah *talking*!" cried Innez, louder.

Floyd shouted back. Then his voice started receding... He was on the move!

Wheeler pulled back from staring at the front of the house and started looking busy. She imagined Floyd rushing out of his mother's bedroom, flying past the sitting room...

Floyd burst onto the veranda above, flew down the steps, across the top yard, and out to the Cut.

Wheeler dropped the broom. She had her eyes on Floyd's zigzagging back. He was dashing uphill, going from side to side.

Fast as she an Donelle does go.

There was a truck, a little flatbed, waiting above, pointing the wrong way on the lane. She recognised the truck.

Old Man Guppy truck dey does drop off people furniture wid, when dey make it. Like d'bad-legged stools in d'kitchen wha Floyd di' make.

Wheeler squatted closer to the ground, squinting up to see…

Who-all an wha else might be up in dat truck.

Arriving at the top of the Cut, Floyd jumped into the cab, and the truck drove off.

Wheeler straightened up. And marvelled.

H-uh, Floyd di' cuss he mudda, *oui*! She in never hear him do dat before.

She cast her eyes around the yard. The ground looked swept enough. She took the broom with her to the lower entrance and gazed at the front elevation of the house, focusing on Innez's bedroom.

"Why ah mus respeck her? Wha ah hav t'care wha she tink?" he di' tell he mudda.

"Ah in finish – Floyd, ah talking!" Tant'Innez di' tell him, fore Floyd di' fly out an go he way!

22

When they first heard the noise of the machine, Wheeler and Donelle had just climbed onto the lane. Wheeler had sensed something on the breeze, a vague churning, a coming and going; something other than the level sound of the water below.

"Y'in hear dat?"

But Donelle seemed to have heard nothing.

The hum of the waterfront played on. The hazy churning dissolved on the tide of the breeze.

Now strolling up to Donelle, Wheeler asked him about what had happened in the house earlier. "Y'in hear dem quarrelling?"

Donelle appeared not to have done. Wheeler sized him up.

He right dere in d'house when it happen. He musta hear!

Maybe he had, maybe he hadn't. Donelle curled his lip, as if to show that he didn't care. He had been shelling peas in the kitchen when Wheeler went in, small pigeon peas for rice-n-peas. Celeste had made her help him before they could get away.

There it was again.

"Y'in hear dat?"

This time he nodded. Yeah, he could hear it. "Wha making it?"

"Ah in know."

Clutching at the tough grass, they worked their way up the slope. The incoming noise seemed to scatter as they climbed. Past the stand of cokey-o-co trees, they edged towards the place where Donelle had tumbled two weeks before.

The cousins negotiated the snake-like roots and hidden dips on the way down, sinking this way and that under the long-legged trees. Neither one mentioned what had happened before.

They paused at the edge of the lane, listening.

Barren fruit trees and meagre shade trees covered the slope on the underside of the road. The sounds of the machine curled and clawed across the open basin at Wheeler and Donelle's feet.

"It coming from out dere!"

They scuffled down the lower slope. The noise ratcheted up a gear. Wheeler looked in the direction in which she had just pointed. The Verdant pasture appeared to their right as they dropped. Sunlight twinkled at their backs before they both melted into the shade.

At the end of the slope, they climbed up from the gutter onto a dirt track and started walking towards the Verdant road. Metal churned against metal as the machine squalled.

There were a number of timber-framed houses alongside the widening track. In defiance of the noise, a woman yelled to a child inside one of the houses.

Out on the road, the source of the iron cry came into view: a massive metal wheel with a little house on top. Not a big truck or a bus or anything she'd seen before. Wheeler studied the noisy vehicle, wondering what it was. Donelle scrunched up his forehead.

The steamroller shuddered and crunched. A slow-drifting current of dust and sound circled the air. A man sat in the high hooded house with the two-ton wheel bristling below. Donelle pointed away to the right, shading his eyes against the dust and then pinching his nose. Overcome by dust and noise Wheeler nodded. She was unable to hear what he was saying.

A group of women were sashaying along the exposed roadbed, balancing large wooden trays on their heads. They tipped the contents of the trays onto the ravaged surface. A bare-chested man shoved and levelled out the chipped stones, pushing a long-handled screed from the edge of the road. Another group of women were headed the other way, carrying empty trays.

Wheeler started sneezing.

Further along the road still more women, bent and stooped, replenished the trays from pointed mounds of stone. The stone-carriers positioned coils of coloured cloth on their heads. Dipping, they hefted the heavy trays onto one another's heads.

Wheeler's eyes watered.

She di' see country women kerry provision on dey head in d'market. But never stone.

Donelle tapped her arm as the mighty steamroller approached.

The roadside screeder walked back, having completed his levelling. Black and grey stones flooded the roadbed near where they stood. Noise and dust and stench bludgeoned the air as the bawling iron wheel grew close, flattening the stones.

Unable to hear one another, both Donelle and Wheeler pointed, explaining to each other what was happening, the ground trembling and Donelle lifting a corner of his shirt to his nose.

There was a man visible to the rear of the roller, a red bandana covering his lower face. He was spraying a fine mist of tar, sealing the newly flattened road surface. The iron wheel wobbled.

Swivelling round in his cab, the driver peered down from his high hooded house at the two shrunken figures on the side of the road. He gestured to them. Donelle waved in response.

The driver reared up on his high horse and threw his fist, his soundless mouth opening and closing. "Get d'hell outa here!"

23

Stewpeas with fish and rice. Or stewfish, okra and rice-n-peas. They ate fish every day: swordfish, saltfish, snapper; barracuda, flyfish, sprat that Innez or Floyd brought home during the week. Fish every day but Sunday, when they ate the chicken Celeste had killed the previous day. Today they'd had rice-n-peas, stewed chicken and sweet fried plantain, which Wheeler liked. Soon after lunch Adele had called for Wheeler, so she could wash her hair.

Sitting naked inside the concrete sink, cross-legged, Wheeler complained, "Why ah hav t'wash meh hair?"

Adele rolled her eyes and shook her head. She glanced over to the church clock as if seeking strength from somewhere. She then cupped the carbolic soap, lathered it between her palms. "Ah mean it," she said. "If Donelle warnt t'go dem kinda place, le' him go by heself!" There had been tar stains on Wheeler's dress when she returned home, iron wheels the height of houses in her dreams.

"Y'bunning m'eye!" Wheeler complained.

After rinsing Wheeler's hair, Adele slathered the slithery insides of an aloe leaf onto her head.

"Y'hutting meh head. Ah in like how dat taste!"

After washing, next came the pain of combing out Wheeler's hair. Which Adele left to Hesta.

Sporting three rough and ready plaits, Wheeler emerged on the veranda, two aggrieved slits where her eyes should be.

Why dey in jus trim she hair like Donelle an dem?

Wheeler spotted Jonathan and Donelle heading down the Cut, dressed once more in their church clothes. "All-you wait!" she cried. But the brothers were already a good way down. She went after them, feet skimming section after section of the narrow steps. "Whey all-you going?"

"We going by we farda," Donelle answered, the words swirling behind him.

"How… how come all-you going?"

"We does go sometimes." He slowed down a little at the turn. Jonathan had kept going, disappearing beyond sight, despite Wheeler shouting.

"Why y'in live wid yer farda?"

"He hav he udda chil'ren t'worry bout."

"Wha time all-you coming back?"

No answer. Donelle scuttled down the remaining tiers. "Ah in know," he finally said.

"How come y'in know?"

By the time she reached the bank overlooking Russell Street, there was no trace of Jonathan. Just Donelle racing past the cinema gate.

*

Wheeler crawled back up the Cut, the fiery afternoon sun her only companion. An odd sense of loss accompanied her as she climbed. Whatever energy source had powered her on the journey down was now depleted. The shadow of her three jagged plaits fell part in the bushes, part on the ground.

Dey going by dey farda. Dey in waiting.

Lifting her head, she soon lowered it as bolts of sunlight struck her eyes. Sweat creaked in the soft inner folds of her elbows. Part way up, the concrete house peered down, its once yellow walls bleached white. The endless melting glass windows watched her as she inched back home. Wheeler walked off the Cut at the bottom entrance. The house seemed quieter already as she strolled along the front. Sunday, the hottest of all days. Sunday afternoon, the cruellest, loneliest time of all.

After taking a drink at the concrete sink, Wheeler headed for the shade at the back of the house. Passing the kitchen doorway, she spied Floyd seated at the kitchen counter.

"Who dat?"

She pressed on up the rocky yard.

Floyd wasn't responsible f'her. She di' do d'punishment he mudda di' giv her. Since den she in do nutting wrong—

Louder: "Who dat? *Come back here*… Y'deaf?"

Wheeler stiffened. She stood at the open doorway, having turned round on the bumpy yard.

"Y'deaf?" Floyd sat hunched over a plate of food at the counter by the bottom of the stairs. "Wha y'doing out dere?"

Wheeler turned towards the brass spigot. "Ah jus… Ah jus come from d'sink," she said, arm held out, pointing.

"Y'in forget d'water, Floyd?"

Wheeler's arm lowered at the sound of Innez's voice.

Casting a lazy eye at the high ceiling, Floyd started cleaning his teeth, chipping away with his tongue.

Wheeler stared, trying to understand him.

He mudda di' call him, why he in going?

Floyd looked at her. "Go. Take a glass o' water up d'stairs."

Wheeler remained where she was in the yard.

He di' put her in trouble once before. She in going.

Floyd grinned to himself. "Y'tink ah carnt *make* you? Celeste carnt help you, y'know." He shot to his feet. The stool flung back from under him.

Wheeler stopped breathing. She had the sense of being lifted and carried into the kitchen. She retrieved an upturned glass, filled it with water, hands shaking. Edging past Floyd, she headed upstairs, doing as she was told.

She got out of the house afterwards, through the sitting room and the veranda, her short legs struggling to find a rhythm down the concrete slope on the terraced side of the house. Wheeler's small lips quivered. She dipped her head. She was nursing a sore heart.

Everyting di' change.

She was no longer beyond the reach of Floyd.

Y'mudda in leave y'wid Floyd, she sister di' say.

She heard Adele and Hesta joking at the back of the house.

She dint warnt t'go an sit wid dem.

Not knowing who or what she could trust, Wheeler didn't know what she should do.

The sloped concrete strip led to the outside entrance to Celeste's bedroom. Wheeler came to a halt and looked in. Celeste was lying on the bed. She had never gone inside her aunt's bedroom and wouldn't go there now. A grown person's private place wasn't somewhere she would enter.

Less dey sen f'her an she in trouble.

Celeste carnt help you, y'know!

Wheeler stared at the long, dark legs lying limp on the faded bed sheet. She remembered Celeste teaching her how to swizzle the eggs then letting her swizzle them by herself. Remembered Celeste telling her to stop coming in the kitchen to help. This made her heart hurt more.

Celeste shifted a leg. Wheeler moved away.

At the back of the house, her sisters were seated together on low protruding rocks: Adele, head drooping down, writing in an exercise book; Hesta beside her, tipped forwards, an airmail letter on her lap. Neither looked up as Wheeler went to join them. It seemed that at times her sisters would form a circle that didn't include her. She sat down: feet in the gutter, eyes on Adele.

Adele scratched at the exercise book with a pencil rubber. She blew away the scraps then started murmuring under her breath, "Y'not t'worry. We all doing well. But we in get d'money y'sen. It in come yet…"

Adele's lips stopped moving.

Wheeler's eyes remained on Adele once she started writing. After she started mumbling again, Wheeler interrupted her.

"Ah taut y'say we mudda in leave us wid Floyd?"

Adele's head shot up. "Wha— He hit you?"

No… he in hit her. Dat in d'point. D'point was… He di' start treating her like Donelle an dem!

Wheeler looked away to the volcanic yard where late-afternoon light tumbled inside the trees.

Adele had returned to drafting her letter. Head cocked to the side, she pressed into the exercise book with the tall pencil. Hesta swiped left to right with her index finger, reading the blue airmail letter in her lap.

"Why we mudda hav t'go in Ingland? Why she hav t'go?" asked Wheeler.

Adele sighed. "Times hard. E'rybody doing wha dey hav to—"

"When she sending f'—"

Adele frowned. "And annuda ting… *Stop* asking Linky if he can come up here an play wid all-you!"

Wheeler sat up.

"He working hard t'help out he mudda. H-he carnt go knocking about d'place wid you an Donelle."

Though Wheeler's mouth fell open, no words came out.

Adele gestured to Hesta. "Read d'letter again."

Smoothing the crisp airmail letter, Hesta read out loud: "It still cold. Ah in meet much people from home. The place so lonely…"

Adele shook her head. "No. Further down."

"Ah saving a little bit by bit. Help yer sister wid she homework. Ah working hard an tinking bout all-you."

"But she hav t'*sen* f'us. She hav t'sen f'us *now*!" Wheeler insisted.

"She sending f'us when she *able*!" Hesta snapped. "Some people leave dey chil'ren an dey in *never* look back. Is dat what y'warnt? Y'warnt *dat* t'happen?"

Wheeler lowered her head.

She in hav no farda, she in hav no mudda. She in hav nobody… dey mudda in sending f'dem.

Losing faith in her mother, resenting Hesta, Wheeler felt alone in the world. She remembered Christmas shopping with her sisters, being in the Back Street bakery eating bakes-n-souse.

Eyes on the ground, Wheeler drifted away. Any closeness she'd felt to Adele and Hesta since their mother's departure was now gone.

Later, on their return from visiting their father, Jonathan climbed the stairs to their mother's bedroom. Donelle settled in his place on the stairs. Wheeler had planned to ask him about their visit. Instead she heard herself say, "Floyd tink he can treat me jus like all-you."

Donelle glanced up. To Wheeler's disappointment there was no look of surprise on his face.

"Meh sister say me mudda in leave us wid him," Wheeler insisted. "But…" Her voice cracked. "He tell me… take d'water upstairs and if ah in take it… he goan make me."

Donelle still seemed unmoved.

'Sif he *tink* she in diffrent. 'Sif… he *always* di' tink she like Jonaton an him!

Soon Floyd would be coming down for supper. Donelle searched the upper landing. "Y… y'in *not* do it?"

Wheeler kept her face turned from him.

"Y'dint answer him back?" Donelle sounded alarmed. The kerosene stove ticked in its enamel skin.

Wheeler glared at Donelle, closed her eyes and shook her head.

"Long as y'in say nutting."

24

Wheeler continued to puzzle over what had happened: Donelle not reacting the way she thought he would, Adele seeing nothing wrong in what Floyd had done.

"He tell me go upstairs, else he goan *make* me. Why y'in tell Tant'Innez?"

Adele had responded with a slight shrug.

Surprised by Donelle, let down by Adele, Wheeler thought of little else.

On the way to school, as if sensing her sister's state of turmoil, Adele told Wheeler something she had not shared with her before. Climbing towards the police signal box, she gestured to a group of younger convent girls, their adoring eyes fixed on her.

They lowered their heads as Adele looked their way.

Wheeler glared at the knot of girls.

She in see why she should look at dem. Dey d'same gyuls does look at she sister all d'time. Two o' dem di' carrying dey canteen wid dey lunch. She in see nutting different. Why she mus look at dem?

"Dey does hav childish crush on people," Adele explained.

"Prefects, older gyuls... people dey like."

Wheeler sneered.

Adele sighed. "Why y'skinning-up y'face?" Changing the subject, she said, "Y'not helping Tant'Celeste in d'mornings again?"

Wheeler shook her head. "She say ah musn't come down no more."

Something came into Adele's face, a calculation of sorts. "If Tant'Celeste say y'musn't come down, den do wha Tant'Celeste say."

Going home for lunch, Wheeler gave Donelle a side-on look.

He di' let her down – an not f'd'first time. He only trouble bout heself.

As if reading Wheeler's mind, Donelle shrunk away. His thin neck was oiled with sweat. Then, nearing the turn, he brought up the subject of Floyd himself.

"He does only hit people if dey in do wha he say. Else..." Donelle broke off, a hint of recollection in his eyes. "Or else if dey in do it fast enough."

Wheeler kissed her teeth. "Sch-ups!"

Just then a familiar figure appeared near the top entrance. Geraldine walked onto the Cut, heading the other way. When Wheeler next looked, their aunt had paused, as if catching her breath. She had disappeared into the steep distance before Donelle and Wheeler reached the house.

Walking in, Wheeler asked, "Tant'Geldine looking f'us?"

"No," Celeste answered, "she jus gone." Celeste stood at the iron pot, hand on her waist, ready to serve up another plate of rice.

First to make it home, Jonathan leapt up with his empty plate.

"Bwoy, why y'always rushing y'food?" Celeste brandished the serving spoon at his head. Jonathan ducked and laughed, teeth white and large and even. After washing his spoon and plate, he cruised past Wheeler and ran up the stairs.

Having slipped her school bag under the counter, Wheeler took a plate from her aunt and climbed to her usual place.

A small schooner sat on the other side of the bay. A distant figure was dragging a broom or mop along the deck. Wheeler gazed down at the kitchen window, seeming to focus on nothing and nowhere.

Is not we fault how Floyd does kerry on, she told herself. *In matter wha Donelle say.*

Donelle returned from the lavatory and Celeste handed him his plate. She returned the lid to the round iron pot, shooing away a circling fly.

Unable to stop herself, Wheeler's eyes lingered on Celeste.

We mudda di' use t'cook f'us fore she go t'work.

Wheeler recalled the rumble of her mother cooking in the early morning. Half-asleep, getting out of bed, she would meander to the kitchen and trail after her mother as the preoccupied figure twisted about.

"All-you hav cou-cou and okra f'all-you lunch… an curry fish," said her mother in her soft voice.

Wheeler would give her an involuntary, sleepy nod as her mother hurried out of the house. Climbing out of bed again an hour later, she could never remember what her mother had said.

Her attention returned to the lunchtime meal on her plate – a small serving of snapper plus okra and rice. Wheeler held the severed fish head between her fingertips. She bit into the flesh at the neck.

Hesta strolled in. Soon Adele would appear. Picking a small fishbone from her mouth, Wheeler's thoughts were of neither of them. Her rueful eyes landed on Celeste as her aunt strolled out to the yard.

Dey mudda in dere t'cook f'dem now.

After washing her plate, Wheeler went and sat next to Donelle on the lower stairs. The sizzle and crack of the lunchtime news broke in overhead.

Somebody di' turn on d'radiogram in d'sitting room… Who?

Donelle looked away.

Wheeler kept her eyes on him. Only Floyd or Innez were allowed to play the radiogram.

"Is not y'mudda." He mudda di' come in by d'kitchen, when she come f'she lunch.

She studied the folds on Donelle's lowered eyelids.

"Floyd musta come home," she said.

No word from Donelle. Wheeler ran her eyes down the side of Donelle's troubled face.

"Is not we fault how Floyd does kerry on," she said.

25

Saturday morning, Wheeler went downstairs to help Celeste. She'd heard her aunt's voice overriding the noise of the chickens, the heckling cluck a warning and a lure. She persuaded herself that Celeste might make time for her in the kitchen as she'd done before.

At the top of the stairs, Wheeler heard Floyd's mocking words, as if he were standing beside her on the landing: *Celeste carnt help you!* She glanced back at Floyd's bedroom.

She di' miss she ant, she di' miss seeing her scrub shit off d'eggs and not breaking dem. She di' miss her looking out d'window telling bout how tings used to be.

"Time was dey di' hav man-o'-wars down on d'dock – *dee*-mans! – carrying gun an ting," Celeste had said one morning, shoving the heavy cocoa pot onto the stove.

Wheeler remembered the cocoa pot rocking, remembered Celeste's thin arm pointing.

"Dey di' raise up submarines right *dere* – out in d'sea."

They had gazed out together at the empty harbour, she and Celeste. Wheeler longed for Celeste to be as she was then.

Now Tant'Celeste di' treat her like she does treat e'rybody else.

Wheeler came level with the doorway and a clear view of the yard. There was no sign of Celeste. Out in the yard, the Rhode Island hens moved like one: heads down feeding, a black and brown scrum with twitching flecks of red. They scuffled and pecked and nudged one another.

She sat on the stairs, waiting.

A slender sailing boat was moored alongside Wharf Road. There were more little fishing boats around the bay than usual, as well as a showering of seagulls. The longer Wheeler waited, a strange harmony seemed to emerge between the strident squawks of the gulls and the humble clucking of the fowls.

Celeste swept out of the bushes. She was holding the feed bucket at her waist as though primed against attack. She appeared prickly and ready to be annoyed; her eyes followed every quick move that the chickens made.

Seeing her cut into the yard, Wheeler's courage and hope started to dissolve.

Hesta's words found their way to Wheeler's ears: *Celeste ain yer mudda!* She felt a sudden need to use the lavatory. The urge became intense.

Wheeler darted towards the corridor under the stairs.

After breakfast, the usual round of chores got under way. Celeste gestured to Jonathan and Hesta: *Come.*

150

This week it was Hesta's turn to buy messages with Jonathan on Wharf Road. Standing at the outdoor sink, finished scrubbing her Keds, Wheeler looked up.

Jonathan slouched into the crook of the counter. Hesta strolled up and faced their aunt. Wheeler listened as Celeste told them what to buy, where, how much to spend and what to leave out.

"Buy d'tania in d'market. Don't buy it in d'shop. We hav enough kerosene, don't buy coals."

"But we could get tania by Marshall and dem—"

"If all-you see fish, buy it," said Celeste.

Wheeler stripped the laces from her sisters' Keds. Her eyes drifted to the kitchen window again, to Hesta and Jonathan.

Every time one o' dem dey di' try an interfere wid wha dey ant di' say – talking bout dey could go here, dere or some udda place – Tant'Celeste di' ignore dem. Or jus turn vex!

Wheeler marvelled at her own lucky escape earlier in the day: she di' lucky she di' run under d'stairs an stay out Tant'Celeste way!

Late afternoon, the heat unending. A hot, static day. A dull cloud sat miserable and low above the bay, unshifting.

Wheeler started climbing the volcanic slope.

"Wait, na!"

She glanced at Donelle perched to the side of the outdoor sink, the back pocket of his shortpants unstitched, hanging. He flicked his hand through the trickle of warm water from which – open-mouthed, tongue lapping – Wheeler had just taken a drink.

Flicking he hand waiting f'd'water t'turn cool. D'water good enough.

She dabbed the back of her wrist against her damp chin and waited. In the kitchen her sisters and Innez drifted back and forth, back and forth, sleepwalking through the various stages of bread-making.

Donelle cupped the running water to his lips. Wheeler started moving on. Part way up the slope, she lifted her eyes on hearing a sudden whack on a radio; a sudden whack followed by a ticklish crackle of applause. That was all Wheeler heard. Donelle picked his way up behind her from about three yards down.

Wheeler headed on out towards the Cut, then looked back and slowed down. Donelle was standing in the slender shade at the back of the house, no longer following. Seeming to have heard something other than the whack of a cricket ball, other than applause, he had his eyes trained on an overhead window. She stared at him.

Wha he doing?

She went and joined him.

Crinkling up one side of his face, thinking, Donelle said, "He hav a woman in dere."

Before anything else could be said, Floyd's face appeared at the window, staring down at them. "Wha all-you doing

152

back dere?"

Two blank faces looked up at the figure in the window, spellbound.

Eyes swaying from one to the other, Floyd tipped out from the window and whispered, "*Sho-oo!*"

The spell broken, Donelle and Wheeler hurtled in different directions. They crashed into one another. They scarpered clear of the window towards the deep dark bushes, getting away from Floyd.

Wheeler stopped.

As frightening as Floyd was…

…she dint warnt t'go in dere.

Donelle rushed in. She swung round, hurried after him. A brassy, metal taste flourished inside her mouth. Her bottom lip stung.

"Y'make me bite meh lip—"

"Ah make you bite y'lip? *Hush* up!"

Wheeler scanned around in the terror of the bushes.

Jonaton di' say dey hav snake in here: *Stay out d'bush dat side o' d'yard.*

Hesta had contradicted Jonathan: "Snake in int'rested in dem!"

Wheeler hesitated… she couldn't see her feet!

"Geddown," Donelle hissed from somewhere.

W-hey he…?

Wheeler fell to the ground. Pockets of underwater light played overhead. Yellow and green vines climbed up to the heavens. Everything grown over everything else. She hugged her knees close to her chest, shrank in on herself. Then, peeking out from the corners of her eyes, she started searching around. She marvelled at where she'd found herself: crowded in by bushes, with no way of knowing if snakes were coming. Quiet in the trees nearby, as if the vegetation held its breath. Sweet, tender birdsong reached her ears from the distance. The sound of a gurgling chicken next. But not the sound of someone coming.

She dragged her attention back to where she was. Young lime-green lizards rustled the leaves on the ground, slithering towards her. Watching them disappear, Wheeler twisted towards the remnants of the back wall—

Floyd!

She spied between the trees. Could see no one.

Floyd in following dem. He not following dem here.

She wondered if Donelle thought the same thing.

Whey he is?

She touched her finger to her bit lip. Donelle was nearby. She could sense but couldn't see him. "Wha y'hear?" she asked, setting aside her annoyance with him.

"Y'in hear he hav a woman in he bedroom laughing?" he asked, to the side of her.

Wheeler thought back.

She di' hear people clapping on d'radio. She di' hear d'cricket bat hit—

"Ah in hear."

This brought Donelle clear of the bushes. He regarded Wheeler with contempt, shook his head then disappeared.

She in hear.

Feeling foolish compared to Donelle, Wheeler glanced at her index finger. There'd been a bloodstain when she'd taken the finger away from her lip. She stared at the smudge again.

"Don-elle?" Wide tree trunks blocked her view; the creepers were thicker, the trees bigger than out by the Cut. "Le' we go."

She couldn't see him. Wheeler wondered if he still thought Floyd was coming, or whether Donelle just wanted to stay in the bushes...

...t'show he in fraid.

She remembered that the bushes came awake at night with croaking and hissing. An ugly crapeau jumping.

So whey dey gone now?

The terrifying answer came: Dey *right* here.

"Ah *going!*" Wheeler jumped up and reached for the crumbling remains of the back wall. Donelle forced his way out, one arm first.

She fumbled over the broken wall. There was a stony dip pointing to where the land rose. The vegetation grew looser in the hollow. Dry stalks came away in her hands. Laying her palms on the ground, Wheeler manoeuvred her way to the next level.

Sunlight played in the trees overhead and along the

line of the road. The same trees she'd see from the top lane, their canopies floating like flat-headed lilies on the underside of the road. The sunlit side of the family house came into view as Wheeler glanced back.

Donelle was behind her. He was in the hollow, tackling ground Wheeler had already covered. There was frustration in his eyes, anger on his sweating upper lip. As she made her way high above the shadowy back of the house, she looked again.

She di' take she time.

Donelle was snatching and grabbing at the curved bell of land, slipping and falling onto his side.

Afterwards, they stared down from the spindly shade offered by the grass on the edge of the Cut. The same low-hanging cloud darkened the afternoon. The near corner of the bay lay burdened under its motionless weight. The shadow of the grass played against the side of her face.

Wheeler ran her tongue around her bottom lip, where a slippery bump had started forming. "Floyd in worrying wid us," she said. She returned her tongue to her mouth.

Below them, the family house had disappeared under the lie of the land, roof and walls and windows no longer visible. And Floyd's bedroom.

As she'd made her way across the parched and crumbling ground, the corrugated roof of the house had spread below her. And Wheeler had stopped, unprepared for what she saw. Prior to this, she'd only ever seen the sides and corners of the roof, with the rest of it sinking from view whenever she climbed the Cut. An extended dingy cloth, the vast discoloured roof was crimped and faded to pink and rust in places, or no colour at all. It was a curious view of the house, which had now disappeared under the cover of the land.

She brushed a blade of grass from her ear.

Having struggled and slipped in the hollow, Donelle had become agitated crossing above the roof. He'd slammed and kicked and cussed at the crumbly, shifting soil each time his flip-flops slipped off.

Wheeler sneaked a peek at him where he sat to the back of her. She fiddled with the dusty toe -pegs on her rubber flip-flops.

She di' get dust in she slipper too, but she in cuss. She in cuss when dey di' bump one anudda eida.

"Floyd in worrying wid us," Wheeler said. "He in coming chasing us."

Donelle glared towards the disappeared house. He didn't look convinced.

One of the little kids from lower down had started climbing the Cut. Donelle's eyes jerked up. He slung his arm. "Go on back *h-o-me!*" he shouted.

The small boy teetered sideways, then started walking down. He kept checking behind him as he went. After the boy had vanished, the Cut felt empty and still, the boy's disappearance having created a kind of emptiness.

Wheeler's eyes gravitated towards Donelle. "Wha wrong wid Floyd?" she asked. "Why he does get on like dat? He in like Tant'Celeste." Then, after a pause, she added: "Why he in like all-you?"

Donelle did not answer her. His tormented expression seemed to draw him deeper into himself.

"Floyd in like *nobody*," Adele had said. Wheeler no longer thought that was true. Her thoughts took her back to the house. She wondered if her sisters were still down in the kitchen, baking, if the radio was still playing. She wondered if the woman was still in Floyd's bedroom.

"He dint *always* use t'not like her." Donelle's voice was soft and surprising. "He don't like her *now*."

Wheeler leaned nearer. "Why he does hit all-you?"

Later Donelle would say that Floyd didn't *always* push them around. Or hit them. Now, though, he muttered, "Cause he bigger dan us."

Wheeler turned her head away, stumped by what she saw next. Small teardrops ran down Donelle's face. Though he strained against it, his forehead and jaw trembling, it seemed he couldn't stop himself from crying.

That night there was an unusual atmosphere in the kitchen, a mood unlike any Wheeler had sensed before. Waiting for her supper, she watched Adele and Celeste.

Adele wafted alongside the edge of the counter, carrying

a tray of nipple rolls: slim finger rolls with a teat on each end. She placed a nipple roll on every plate. There was a leftover sense on Adele's face of something having happened. A look on Celeste's face, too.

Like she di' know sumting she in warnt t'know.

And above the undertone, intermittent bursts from Panorama Steelband. Nine more days to carnival, and the first of the Saturday night rehearsals had begun. Swirly sounds wound their way inside Wheeler's puzzled brain like the twirling lights sinking inside the bay.

Hesta came in from the yard. Celeste flicked round and gave her a discouraging look. Hesta twisted her face and appeared to grumble to herself.

The room smelled of the usual Saturday night jumble: loaves of bread cooling in the warm night air, a little bit of kerosene, cocoa and saltfish souse – though now with something sombre in between.

After collecting her cocoa and her plate, Hesta went out without speaking.

"Whey we supper?" Wheeler mumbled, watching Hesta leave.

At last Adele gestured to Jonathan to come and collect his plate. He then gestured to Wheeler and Donelle.

As Wheeler strolled back, Jonathan shrugged as if to say *Ah in know eida*, chomping the teats off his nipple roll. Now Floyd was at band practice, he had parked himself in his brother's usual place.

A harsh note sounded.

"Bwoy, when y'planning t'bring up meh food?"

Wheeler watched Donelle's body rock in response to his mother's raucous cry.

He di' seem awright til den.

As Donelle climbed up the stairs, she gave him a sympathetic look.

Peeling off her day clothes, part-naked, Hesta grumbled. "Doing he biznis in he bedroom, wid he mudda in d'house... An he *ant* in d'house." Her voice was full of condemnation and excitement.

"Taking on he mudda when she tell him don't bring no woman in here... Man hav a woman upstairs. We jus downstairs, *oui*!"

"Is wha Donelle say," Wheeler mumbled, part thinking, part talking to herself.

Glancing at one another, the older girls drew near as Wheeler slid her nightdress over her head. Surfacing, she shied away.

"Wha he say?"

"Donelle di' say he hear sumting. He hear a woman laughing. In Floyd room."

"When he hear her?"

Wheeler sank onto the mattress. "When we coming back up from d'sink."

"Wha time all-you come back from d'sink?" urged Hesta.

She in know.

Hesta's voice altered, a look of fascination coming into her face. "When else you di' hear dem?"

"Ah in hear dem—"

"He in hear dem before...?" Hesta drew closer still. "He in tell y'nutting else?"

Adele reached out and touched Hesta's arm. "W-hat?" Hesta protested, glancing over her shoulder, shrugging off Adele. "Little kids can be tricky," she insisted, as Adele steered her away.

26

The following morning, after church, as the sisters changed out of their church clothes, Innez yelled for Adele from across the landing.

Coming back into the room, eyes lowered, Adele said, "We hav t'go an see Miss Eadie. She hav a stroke. She in hospital." Adele appeared to be in shock.

Seated on the floor, unbuckling her church shoes, Wheeler asked Adele, "Wha-t's a ... *str-o-ke*? Whas dat?"

Hesta took it upon herself to explain. "A stroke is sumting people does get."

Miss Eadie had been their neighbour when they lived in town. Wiry and strong, her small, crinkled face was furrowed and lined. Wheeler imagined Miss Eadie was as old as anybody could be. She still tended her own kitchen garden and took a firm hand to her flock of fowls. Wheeler recalled their neighbour's stringy voice singing in the mornings in the concrete yard a few steps down from their own."Rock of Ages". Together, the cackle of the hens and Miss Eadie's voice would tell Wheeler it was time to get up once her mother left for work.

"Who looking after she chicken?"

"Sch-uu! Miss Eadie chicken can look out f'deyself," Hesta said.

From the bedroom window, Wheeler would watch the chickens surround Miss Eadie, who kept on singing. She brought to mind the steep chicken coop, the tiled orange rooftop on Miss Eadie's house. She tried, but was unable to picture Miss Eadie in hospital.

After lunch, dressed once more in their church clothes, Wheeler and her sisters set off. St Catherine's Hospital was located in the oldest part of the capital, on the edge of the headland behind the fort. They descended into the gleaming, white waste of the afternoon, the Cut deserted, the glinting sun bearing down on them.

"Whey y'going?" Hesta hollered back at Wheeler part way down.

"Ah warnt Donelle to come wid us."

Adele called up, "He hav t'go by he farda."

They carried on down.

The bottom road ran empty of any visible sign of life, with people hiding in their homes, resting. There were tiny ripples in the pitch-dark shade – kids giggling.

Wheeler lagged behind her sisters, going past the line of row houses. The heat outside the shade continued to harden and struck the side of her face as it rose off the surface of the road. Where the line of houses ended up ahead, the afternoon sky continued to whiten. As she emerged into the open, the angry sun looked down from its box and shouted at her head.

At the top of Russell Street, she stuck close to the shade at the edge of the road. Then, getting ahead of her sisters, Wheeler turned left onto Church Street, where she spotted other children like her, out on Sunday visits. Kids dressed in their church clothes: teenage girls in drop-waist dresses, younger girls in frocks, big tie-bows in the front, boys in ironed shirts and khaki shortpants. Wheeler stared down at herself.

She church dress di' getting too small – she mus tell Adele.

Having gotten ahead of her sisters, she now waited for them. She stared down Market Hill. Not a soul in town. Two vehicles on the road. She looked away from the tall wooden houses lining the hill towards the unseen streets to her right. The house where they'd lived wasn't far away.

Dey carnt walk past it, Adele di' say.

Dey hav people living in dere now, Hesta di' say.

Wheeler didn't think that was a good enough reason. *Dey hav people living everywhere!*

Adele and Hesta seemed to float on the wavy electric air as they climbed the last of Russell Street. Veering left, Wheeler walked on without them.

Old red-brick houses stood on either side of Church Street, green shutters closed, in this once grand section of the capital. Here and there the houses' crumbling, powdery brickwork gave way to mortar patches the size of continents.

The Anglican church tower rose to Wheeler's left – enormous this close up! Disturbed by the size of it, Wheeler stood still. Two outsized faces confronted her, more dented than she remembered. The clock's hands were spindly and warped. It was the same clock she'd seen as she'd looked up from the house in town, the same viewed from across the bay. Still…

Wheeler looked over her shoulder. She wondered where her sisters were. She turned her back to the clock.

Adele and Hesta approached in their sun-bleached dresses, hemlines below their knees. They advanced at a chatting pace, both talking at the same time, unhurried. Wheeler sucked on the little bump on her lip, waiting. She wondered what they were saying.

Hesta came to a halt, talking over Adele. Head to one side, Adele kept on talking. Both fell silent as Wheeler drew close. "Before y'start," warned Adele, "we *not* going in town."

Wheeler glanced down at the grid of streets in between the houses, at the pale brick buildings, the clay-tiled roofs.

Not dat. She hav udda tings t'tell her.

"When ah go get meh new church dress?"

"When d'money come—"

"Is Miss Eadie goan die?"

"Ah… ah… in know if she goan die." Adele appeared shaken all over again. Her voice choked. "She on'y hav a stroke is all. People does change sometime," she muttered, "after dey hav a stroke."

"Why dey does change?"

Why? Looking away from Wheeler, Adele turned to Hesta for support.

Hesta's hard eyes fixed Wheeler with a look. And she continued to glare… until Wheeler walked away.

On Old Fort Road, they started smelling the engine of the hospital, the terse, emphatic smell of disinfectant. Wheeler ran up the grassy incline. She took a drink at an iron standpipe outside the fort walls. As she straightened up, a small version of the waterfront appeared to her left, with miniature terraces and a tiny cinema building. The thoughts in Wheeler's mind fell away. She stared in wonder at the shrunken view. As her eyes ranged in the other direction, paper birds scattered like confetti in front of the long dock buildings. Water competed with land. Sunlight brightened unknown straits further out to sea, to her right.

Wheeler pulled back. She squinted inland. Tiny trees stood alongside red-roofed houses above the cinema building, including the white house she now called home.

The two-storey hospital was brownish yellow, the colour of rotting cocoa pods left out in the sun. Patients and visitors sat on benches on the first-floor veranda that ran the length of the pavilion-style building. Everyone seemed cloaked in the stench of disinfectant. The men's wards were on the ground floor, the women's on the top floor.

Climbing the outer steps, the sisters peered at the wards below. There were men in bandages, one of them bare-chested, with his leg in traction pointing towards the other side of the ward.

Her sisters went ahead of her into one of the wards. Wheeler hovered at the open doorway. There were two rows of beds, with a wide linoleum passage down the middle. There were visitors sitting and standing to the sides of the grey iron beds. Some of them turned to stare at the girl standing part-in, part-out, a large bow at the front of her dress.

Adele gestured for Wheeler to *come on*. But Wheeler did not. Instead she decided to run.

She dint warnt t'see Miss Eadie, she dint warnt t'go in dere. She dint warnt t'see if Miss Eadie di' change.

Later, as her sisters came down from their visit, Wheeler drew herself deeper into the turn of the hospital stairs.

Dey carnt make her go up dere!

"Ah in warnt t'see Miss Eadie," she whimpered. "Y'in goan make me go upstairs."

Hesta walked on by. Adele looked out to the low orange buildings scattered between the dried-out bushes, little convalescent huts stretching away from the hospital. "Le' we jus go home," she said, turning to Wheeler. "Get up off that dutty step."

"Y'not going t'tell Tant'Innez?"

"Why ah goan tell her? Jus come on."

Wheeler took hold of the wooden rails.

She didn't warnt t'see Miss Eadie. She di' warnt everyting t'stay d'same as before dey mudda leave.

"Whey Donelle an dem?"

Overripe with emotion, despite knowing they'd be gone, Wheeler started missing Donelle and Jonathan when she got home.

"Er-*cch!*" The scent of the hospital lingered in her throat.

"Bring down yer homework," Adele said. "Dey in come back yet."

When her sisters went down to the kitchen to start ironing, Wheeler took her homework with her to the bottom of the stairs. She then backed up to the middle step, Donelle's place. Setting herself up over the fat middle step, she muttered, "Wha dey farda warnt wid dem?"

Adele carted the wooden ironing board from under the stairs. As she eased it down, one of the long scissor-legs leapt out. Standing at the stove warming the clothes irons, Hesta swung round, trapping the wayward leg in the underbelly of the ironing board.

Wheeler lowered her head and returned to her homework.

A wave of tangerine sunlight worked its way around the kitchen, revealing the oily patina of the shiny unpainted walls. Adele now stood sprinkling a large pile of school shirts: squeezing then rolling them, stacking them on top of one another for when the irons got hot. The three dirt-brown clothes irons were like miniature sailing boats: pointed at the front and square at the back. Using a tightly wadded rag, Hesta lifted one of the little irons from the kerosene flame. She smoothed it against a clean kitchen cloth. She pressed and smoothed the iron a couple more times, until it ran clear of soot. Then she threw down one of the school shirts and started ironing.

The sisters would take turns prepping the clothes irons and ironing the shirts. They'd clear the kitchen in time for supper and if need be, once the supper things were cleared away, start the prepping and ironing all over again.

Wheeler asked, "Whey we farda gone?"

Adele paused. For a moment she stopped crumpling the remaining school shirts into balls. Then she started again. Hesta puffed herself up with some heavy intakes of breath. Neither she nor Adele spoke.

The ironing board sashayed and sang, its loose leg squeaking. Wheeler stood up and looked set to ask the same question again.

Hesta said, "We in know!"

Then Adele said, "He gone overseas. He in coming back."

"Why he in coming back?"

"Might be he *drung*—" Hesta said.

"We in know dat." Adele turned to Hesta, an exasperated look. "He in drung. We jus in know whey he gone."

Hesta plonked one of the sailing boat irons on the endplate. A sound like spite sliced the air. "Might as well hav drung. He leave an he in *never* look back."

Wheeler sat back down.

The heavy squeak of the ironing board was now the only sound. The angular, fraught face of her mother came to Wheeler's mind. The features of her father remained a blank.

"How he look? Wha we farda look like?" Wheeler's eyes remained on Adele, avoiding Hesta. They had no pictures of their father or their mother.

Hesta flicked the shirt she'd been battering onto its side.

Adele answered, "We farda look jus like all of us: you, me an Hesta."

Hesta shook her head and closed her eyes.

Celeste came in. "All-you ironing now? Is nearly time we start t'cook."

"We know, Tant'Celeste…"

"We trying an finish."

"All-you go by Miss Eadie?" Celeste folded her arms across her chest. "How she doing?"

Finishing rolling up the shirts, Adele glanced at Wheeler. "Ah go tell y'later, Tant'Celeste."

We farda look jus like all of us. Wheeler wondered what

that face might be like.

Hesta face hard, wid nutting nice at all. She di' always looking at her bad.

Wheeler then thought about Adele: *She face in hard – but when she warnt, she could be jus as bad as Hesta.*

Thinking about her own face next to those of her sisters, Wheeler decided her face was all right. Even so, a sense of their father's face never came into her mind.

After the ironing had been cleared away, Donelle and Jonathan returned from their Sunday visit. The two boys stood in the centre of the kitchen, eyes on the kitchen counter. Seated at the counter, Floyd growled, "Wha all-you looking at?"

"We jus come…" Donelle continued staring to where his and Jonathan's supper waited for them. "We jus come," he repeated, unable to conceal his desire to fetch his plate.

"Go upstairs!" said Floyd, adding, "Wha all-you get?"

Jonathan reached inside his shortpants pocket and produced a piece of paper. A brown money bill.

"Go on up!" Floyd gestured to Donelle as well.

27

Wheeler had a visit from her mother. Standing smiling outside their former home, her mother said, "Come."

She held out her hand and they set off towards the bottom of the road. Their long wooden house grew higher and higher in the distance behind them. As they neared the sea wall, the rallying sound of a conch shell filled the air: *Come get y'fish!* Hand in hand, she and her mother hurried across the street.

There were heavy footsteps on shingles behind the sea wall: the sound of the fishermen climbing out of their boats. Wheeler looked down. A man climbed out of a little fishing boat in a brown Sunday suit. He was carrying a grip suitcase. Shirtless men worked around him, landing buckets of fish. He crunched across to the deep stone steps, leading up to the street. A surge of delight coursed through her. They'd seen what they'd come to see.

Wheeler reached for her mother's hand. Turning, she and her dream mother carried on back along Water Street. The man walked on, heading the other way.

She had seen her father's face.

Waking up, Wheeler stared at the high wooden ceiling, remembering the dream. She recalled the moment on Water Street. She carried on staring.

The smile on her face faded. The image of her father's face had disappeared, washed away on the breaking, sifting surface of the sea.

Walking back to school the next day, Donelle looked at Wheeler. "Y'not still missing y'mudda?"

Wheeler's chest seized up. As it happened, she was still thinking about her father.

She was always goan be missing she mudda! "Is... is okay f'you," she managed. "Y'still be missing y'mudda if it was you."

Donelle appeared doubtful. "Ah woulnt be missing meh mudda. She in never do nutting t'help me. She in never do nutting bout Floyd." He strode off, taking the long gutter steps to Mill Street.

Jonathan had been walking alongside them. Wheeler turned her attention to him, hoping for support. Jonathan's sympathetic eyes looked down at her. He did not criticise what his brother had said.

28

Saturday morning, Adele called up for Wheeler to go to the seamstress, to get measured for her church dress.

Leaving the veranda, Wheeler sneered at Donelle.

She in never talking t'him again. She in even *asking* if he can go wid dem, after he rudeness 'gainst she an she mudda.

Donelle was dragging the yard broom outside Celeste's bedroom. He didn't seem to notice Wheeler coming.

How she could tink he she fren – she best fren!

Wheeler marvelled as she walked past him.

She had walked home alone after school, following what Donelle had said. Had raced right up the Cut, not checking to see whether or not he was coming. She'd then watched him leave the house and veer right further down towards Carter Hill.

T'play wid Christopher and he brudda, an all dem udda *likkle* chil'ren.

Adele gestured to her to stand still. She straightened Wheeler's hair ribbon.

The domed sky grew deeper as Wheeler bumped downhill. She was wearing the little church dress that needed replacing, the round armholes squeezing. She would have to be patient after being measured, would have to wait for material to be bought, wait to be fitted. It would take a week or two for the new dress to be ready. No one could afford ready-made clothes.

People were cutting across the cinema yard, others were going up and down the cinema steps. St Catherine's Bay stretched and quivered, quivered and strained like a long blue muscle.

As they passed the open gate, Adele started speeding up, but then slowed down as if remembering she wasn't heading to school.

Wheeler lagged behind. "Why we carnt go in town?"

"Ah told you."

"Why ah carnt get a stripe dress?"

"Ah in say *wha* y'carnt get. It depend… Depend on wha dey hav."

"We in going in town?"

Adele kept walking. She'd already told Wheeler they weren't going to town. And why. "We carnt keep going by Miss Rudy. Dey hav seamstress right round here."

"Why we carnt get d'material? Why we carnt get it now?"

"Ah not going in town. Ah go get d'material anudda time."

"Why we carnt get it now?"

"Why y'not coming?"

Wheeler kept her eyes on the ground, unsure which of her sorrows she would tend first.

She sister di' say not t'worry bout Miss Eadie. Miss Eadie a old lady. Adele di' say, "Jus worry bout yerself. If people ask jus say she doing okay." Now Miss Rudy in making dey clothes no more. Tings di' change.

They turned right onto Lime Street. A pair of girls seated on the front step of a house called out Wheeler's name.

"Why y'in answer? Y'in hear people calling you?"

A few days before, going down Churchway, one of the girls had questioned Wheeler, had put a hand on her satchel: "Wha y'doing in here? Wha school y'does go to?"

Wheeler recognised the girls. Why she mus answer, when dem d'same gyuls dat di' giv her cut-*eye* when she walking home from school?

She had carried on walking, not answering. She carried on walking now.

"Is time y'start make frends wid new people," Adele told her.

Hearing this made Wheeler think of Donelle… when she dint self warnt t'remember he name.

When they arrived at the seamstress's house, a woman rocking a baby came and ushered them in. "Morning."

"Morning," they answered.

"Dat Miss Springer?"

Wheeler followed Adele into the house. A long, sunless corridor pointed them to where they were going. There was a radio playing somewhere. Daylight teetered at the end of the landlocked entrance, as did the leftover smell of a meal.

"Morning."

"Morning…"

Arriving in the spacious back room, Wheeler and Adele nodded half a dozen times to the women seated there, said "Morning" several times more. As well as the nodding women, two figures stood to the side of a sewing machine, one with a mouthful of pins, adjusting a part-finished dress.

"Morning, Miss Springer," said Adele.

"All-you come?" the woman with the pins answered. She spluttered the words.

Adele and Wheeler sat down.

Miss Springer's workroom was a glittery gallery of carnival costumes. The fizz and excitement of afternoon Mas was right there in the long, sunny room.

Wheeler's mood lifted. She di' walk by dis house every day. She dint know dey di' hav so much going on here.

Adele nudged Wheeler. "Stop staring people in dey eye."

"How ah staring people in dey eye?" She didn't know where to look.

The carnival costumes came to Wheeler's rescue. Waves of gold. All kinds of blue and silver and yellow. She shuffled round in her chair, taking a closer look. Blue seas and silver skies on longpants and skirts. Silver sequins getting ready to shine out in the sun. The pageantry and spark of afternoon carnival: men and women, arms around one another, swaggering, wining, midriffs showing.

She squinted at Adele. "Wha dey playing?"

"We playing twenty towsend league under d'sea," said one of the women.

Another said, "All-you in come f'all-you costume?"

Adele shook her head. The profane and pious met. "Ah getting m'sister measured... f'she church dress."

29

Carnival came.

Soft black sky. The darkest, highest point of the night. The moon gone. A blue curve of blackness over the bay. The insect cacophony of the night powering down: a blissful, baffling time.

The fading glow of fireflies. As the household drifted down the Cut, waning yips of insect sounds flew out of the bushes. Separated from her bed, muddled feet carried Wheeler to the street below. There were muffled greetings from faceless shadows along the road. Everyone making their way towards town.

As they approached the police traffic box, the noise from town started reaching them. It mingled with the soft-cut figures drifting along the road.

Descending Market Hill, the sisters reached the mayhem of J'Ouvert Morning. The clatter of saucepans and other homemade instruments, the raw pulse of tyre rims and jack iron declared the rowdy start of carnival. And people. People spilling into the opening at the bottom of the hill, people all across town in the heavy darkness before dawn. Wheeler watched as her sisters and Jonathan melted away in the crowd.

Innez whipped her arm around and grabbed hold of Wheeler, having already snatched Donelle as he tried to follow Jonathan. Bundling them together, she shoved and guided them to the side of the road. They started fumbling up a set of stairs against the side of a house.

They rose above the noise. Wheeler inhaled the wild excitement. She smelled the sweat fermenting over the jam-packed crowd. Carnival bacchanal: blue-black flesh rolling, people hollering, jumping-up wining, letting go of their inhibitions.

"All-you go on up!"

Donelle tripped up the metal steps and grabbed hold of the railings behind Wheeler. She had made up with him, despite all she'd said. They stood together at the top of the steps, waiting for Innez.

She led them through the crowded, dimly lit house.

From a balcony overlooking Market Square, Wheeler and Donelle glanced at one another, their bodies buffeted by arse-shaking women. Grown-up women they both knew from church and Sunday school wining, grining to the different sounds. Wheeler looked around. She thought of Miss Bench wining on a balcony like this, her stern bosom swirling round and round. Or else down in the street.

Action everywhere, syncopated rhythms right across town.

She heard the cry of a conch. The sounds of people laughing, people *roaring*, glanced off the balcony ledge on the way to the black heavens.

In the square opposite, a shadowy herd of country buses stood patient and silent, waiting to take people home. People from Reverie, Shooter's Hill and Mildenhall – from all about – come to play Old Mas in town.

A new confusion. In the street below a half-naked man was parting the crowd. Something like a mask on his head, a sign on his chest.

People jeered and cussed as "The-Prime-Minister" was wheeled by in a rocking bath.

A hollowed-out drumbeat, followed by a waning of the noise—

"Wha happen?"

Wheeler's eyes followed Donelle's.

To the left of the square, shackles broken, chains rattling, a troupe of Jab-Jab emerged in the grey dawn. A blackened regiment of men slicked in tar, molasses and oil. The thump of the drum died down, pushed aside by a harrowing angry chant of "Jab-Jab, Jab-Jab, Jab-Jab!"

Women feinted at the oil-slick bodies, darted then ran away. The regiment pressed on.

The chant of the battalion swelled, taken up by the crowd: "Jab-Jab, Jab-Jab, Jab-Jab, Jab-Jab, Jab-Jab, Jab-Jab, Jab-Jab, Jab-Jab, Jab-Jab, Jab-Jab, Jab-Jab, Jab-Jab, Jab-Jab, Jab-Jab, Jab-Jab, Jab-Jab…"

A blistering sound. Hymn of defiance – the history of enslavement, of resistance, carried onto the streets.

As the battalion drew near, some old barbarity ran ahead of it, piercing a little girl's heart.

Up on the balcony Wheeler fainted, tumbling backwards.

They laid her down on a wicker chaise and started fanning her.

"All-you le' d'chile *breathe*!"

Someone gave Wheeler a cup of water when she came to. The woman stroked Wheeler's head.

Wheeler's eyes searched above the rim of the cup: hands and big faces she in never see before… *and* Tant'Innez face—

Wheeler tried to sit up.

"Lay down dere," hissed Innez. Wheeler's eyes met Innez's impatient glare over the rim of her eyeglasses. "Okay," Innez declared, "she awright now!" And then disappeared.

Other people hurried back to the balcony, following Innez.

Wheeler heard a sudden surge of shouting down in the street. There was a sense of threat everywhere. Nowhere.

There was someone beside her, tall black furniture surrounding him.

"Whey y'bin?"

"Ah in go nowhere!" said Donelle. "Dey tell me t'keep out. Le' y'sleep."

*

The rest of the day was marked by a series of comings and goings, once Donelle and Wheeler got home.

Around eleven o'clock, an unknown man came to collect Floyd.

Sitting by the concrete sink, Wheeler heard someone shouting Floyd's name. She watched as Donelle flew up the yard to the back of the house. He signalled for her to follow him up.

"Floyd! Floyd man."

At the top of the yard, Donelle gestured to the man. "He name Selwyn. He come f'him. Dey hav a pan practice. He come f'him."

Wheeler looked out to the Cut.

A long, easy-flowing figure was striding towards the house. "Man, y'dere?" He leapt towards the veranda steps and disappeared round the side of the house. Floyd had stumbled home drunk after J'Ouvert Morning and had fallen down at least once on the way up to his room.

Starting as little more than a hum, Wheeler could hear the man's voice grow rougher as he urged Floyd to wake up. She heard Floyd cuss him. "Y'warnt me t'*cut* yer tail?"

Jonathan shot his head out of his bedroom window, laughing. There were sounds of a struggle next, in Floyd's bedroom. The sound of something... some*one* tumbling hard. Jonathan pulled back in. Wheeler and Donelle stared at one another.

"Come on, man, le' we go."

More struggling. Floyd cussing. Then Jonathan's face at Floyd's bedroom window as Floyd and his bandmate came struggling round the side of the house. Selwyn was shoving Floyd in front of him. Floyd was still pulling on his shirt, two steelpan sticks standing out of his arse pocket.

Selwyn looked round at Jonathan. "Schu-upes… Bwoy, wha y'standing in dere laughing? Get y'brudda costume, na!"

Jonathan disappeared, then a moment later ran out after them. He handed over a set of clothes. Selwyn seized them with his free hand.

Watching Floyd being steered away, relief rushed into Donelle's face. "He not coming back now til tomorrow. Not coming back til carnival done."

Eating their lunch, they listened to the sounds of the steelband practice. Overlapping reels and runs as individual band players warmed up. Stuttering starts. Mostly stops. Until, as she finished eating, came the reward of hearing the entire steelband blow up.

"All-you stay home," warned Adele. "*Don't* go knocking about. When time come t'go, people in warnt t'come looking f'all-you!"

Wheeler looked to Floyd's vacant place. Jonathan had already gone without her seeing him go. "We jus going by d'—"

"Stay home!"

Wheeler's entire face sank. A catastrophe!

Dey coulnt go nowhere! Dey hav t'stay home til time come t'go.

Together Wheeler and Donelle idled up and down the veranda. Took turns to drift out to the Cut then wander back. Until a few minutes after one, when Panorama's costume band started spilling onto Wharf Road.

"All-you come!" Adele shouted.

It was time to get dressed – somewhere between their best homeclothes and their church clothes – and head down to watch the band set up.

As they arrived on Wharf Road, the arrow-straight stench of greasepaint hit Wheeler's lungs. The swish of crushed taffeta and netting surrounded her. The costume band was taking form.

The court of Captain Nemo filed past, papier mâché weapons bobbing, giant squid trailing behind. Leagues of compliant crustaceans started falling in line. The formation of the band continued theme by theme, section by section.

At the front, the steelpans started playing. A second float of pans was being pushed out by the bread shop gap and onto the road. There were older boys diving in and out, in and out of the sea on the opposite side of the street.

Slow, pulsing music carried between the two sets of steelpans. People had started dancing – Mas players and those watching. Dragging their feet, wining. Donelle and Wheeler shook their waists and started strutting like everybody else. A flatbed truck took up the final position near the back of the procession, topped with silver steelpans swaying.

"Okay, le' we go: *Play Mas!*" The loudspeaker hailed for the Queen of the Band at the front to start moving – a signal for crowds at the back to start hooting: "*Hoo-hoo… Bambalay! Hoo-hoo!*"

Sections of the band started stretching forward: water nymphs and crabs—

Adele pulled Wheeler against her.

—Mermaids and sea lions. The diving boys climbed out from the sea and started dancing.

As the last of the band strutted past, Donelle protested. "How come we in going? Why we not playing Mas?"

"Y'buy a costume? Y'in d'band?" Hesta asked him.

"No."

"Ah taut so… Den y'*carnt* play *Mas*."

Having watched the band set off, Donelle and Wheeler hurried home, through the cinema yard, up the steps, along Russell Street. They ran up the Cut, flew clear past the house, to see the procession from above—

"All-you come back down."

"We in calling f'all-you when we going in town," added Hesta.

Impatience nagged away at Wheeler. The band wasn't

moving as fast as she had expected. There was disappointment in her eyes. A distant movement of colour and echoing steelpan music, Panorama's costume band shuffled along. Taking the longer route around Wharf Road, it would be an hour or more before it made it to town. The band lost its head and then its body behind a long mooring of vessels – sailing boats, a schooner and a raft – where the bay turned.

The cousins sat at the top gazing down: Donelle with his head cupped between his hands, Wheeler palm propped under her tilted chin.

There were slivers of blue and gold in between the vessels. The music wavered then sank, as the last of the steelpans slipped away behind the high-sided raft.

In town, Wheeler paused at the bottom of Market Hill. She looked up at the balcony where she had fainted. Daylight had washed away the events of J'Ouvert Morning. Gone the legions of Jab-Jab, gone the kitchen orchestras. Costume bands now roamed the streets: sunshine, sequins and steelbands.

Adele grabbed her arm. "We not standing here. Come!"

They wormed their way along Queen Street. Crowds now crammed the narrow sidewalks, jiggling, as the swaggering costume bands filled the streets. Bands from Tuillerie, Erskine and LaBasque heading for the grandstand outside town, bands from every district vying for the title "Carnival Road Band 1966".

Inca gods on Queen Street. Oversized papier mâché heads. Steelband players in matching T-shirts and shortpants, gold button tunics. The ripple of steelpan music competed with the swaying, rolling sound of revellers singing.

On the corner of Market Square, Wheeler found herself deposited at the front of the crowd, alongside other children. Her eyes swept up. A soaring metal float was struggling round the turn.

"Back up…"

"Back it up!"

Bare-chested men pulled and shouted at one another, trying to get the wheels in line. All the while the Queen of the Band kept on waving, smiling, at the centre of the float, lavish feather plumes nodding.

The children all reared back as the chassis shuddered forward before straightening out. Afterwards, as the band drifted away, they teased and danced in the pulsing hot space left behind.

Another band approached. A small group of people playing Shango in ceremonial white – white headgear, dresses and longpants. A guide rope was strung from front to back between the band's modest floats, a reminder to onlookers to stay out of the band.

When Panorama finally arrived late in the afternoon, the costumes appeared unfamiliar, despite her having seen them on Wharf Road. The music seemed slower to

Wheeler – her ears had since become used to the faster style of some of the other steelbands. Her puzzled eyes drifted about. They landed on Floyd up on the steelband truck pounding his pans.

The following day, Carnival Tuesday, Wheeler and Donelle watched the band from the lane, not going to the seafront to see it set up.

That night, as the celebrations grew wild, as the wandering steelbands came to a halt all across town, Wheeler and Donelle jumped up at the centre of the band amid the blistering cacophony of the rival steelbands.

30

They climbed the field overlooking the lane, dwarfed by Lent's eerie silence.

Silence out to sea. Silence creeping to the top of the church tower. Silence sweeping the hills from left to right and turning inland. The din of silence, carnival's backdraught. Two days of magic and commotion. Days of wonder and glitz, bewilderment and noise. A strange and wounding dawn.

Wheeler remembered seeing Floyd on the back of the flatbed. She'd looked away and caught sight of a woman who looked like Celeste but was not. It was at that moment that she'd realised that Celeste never went up or down the Cut, never went further than the bushes. Celeste never left home. Having lain unshaped in Wheeler's mind, the realisation about Celeste had taken form in the upended world of carnival.

She came to a halt. A heavy mist fell over her eyes as she recalled what she had figured out.

The discovery about Celeste did not lend itself to being talked about.

She di' try telling Adele. "We ant okay. Stop looking f'confusion," her sister had said. Wheeler now kept her thoughts to herself.

Donelle reclined on the grass, having dropped to the ground at the height of the slope. "Kite season soon come," he yelled.

Schu... she in warnt t'hear dat.

They gazed out. Kite season was over a month away and would mark the end of the Lenten season.

"Is true, it soon come," said Donelle, rising up on his elbows.

Wheeler worked her toe into the ground, not answering. Unearthing a clod of earth, she seized it and chucked it into the open—

Morgan's car pulled onto the lane.

Wheeler stared.

Dusting the seat of his shortpants, Donelle hurried past her, making his way downhill.

Wheeler grabbed hold of one of the shopping bags as Morgan lifted them from the car. "Le' me put it on the ground," he said. Skin as tough as animal hide, he smiled a soft, knowing smile. "All-you kerry dis bag in together."

Donelle and Wheeler both lunged for the bag of provisions. They set off, skinny legs bumping against the wicker bag.

"Mind y'in strain yerself."

One arm held out for balance, Wheeler glanced up.

Geraldine stood at the bottom of the steps, keeping the gate open.

The gate clanged after them as they jockeyed up the steps.

"Wait, na!"

Wheeler felt a steady stretching at the back of her legs, felt Donelle try to outstrip her as they carried the rocking load.

"All-you hav all-you lunch?"

"Yes, Tant'Geldine…"

"…Yes, Tantie Geldine."

Easing down the bag, they stood aside as Geraldine went in. She reached out from the doorway and took the messages from them. "Yer sisters awright?" She lifted the bag to the counter.

Dey does style her off. An push her round!

"Yes, meh sisters awright," Wheeler answered.

Morgan carried in the rest of the bags, leaving them on the counter. The bright painted kitchen shone behind him as he strolled to the refrigerator. Wheeler started thinking about Celeste, pictured her inside the drabness of the other house.

Morgan poured a drink each for Donelle and Wheeler. "We going f'a drive," he said. "All-you warnt t'come?"

Raising his hand, Donelle cried out. "Ah warnta!"

"Me, ah warnta," Wheeler mumbled.

The car smelled of hot machinery, leather and cigarette

ash. Its red upholstery was pleated and warm against Wheeler's skin. The little Hillman bounced about in the hollowed-out sump at the bottom of the lane and then curled uphill. They drove past a slope to their left that was brittle with birdsong. As they levelled out on the back lane, the air became dark, less arid.

Racing away to her left was the bank where Donelle had fallen. Holding on to the window winder, perching up, Wheeler peered across at the Verdant basin, the green expanse of land where the steamroller had brawled and gnarled, where the driver had threatened them from his cab.

As the car swung by, the broad, open basin turned itself around. Donelle pulled back as Wheeler tipped towards him, staring at the swerving, changing view.

At the Guide Hall wall, where the circle of the lane both began and ended, Wheeler glanced at Donelle. He sat with his head resting on the back seat. He was not sitting up, not swivelling round. He had been in the car before. Wheeler let go of the window winder and sat back, embarrassed by her excitement.

So wha if she dint hav a drive in d'car before? Wha if she in know she ant an uncle as good as Donelle? Dint know Uncl'Morgan would let her help if she jus ask.

Geraldine glanced out of the side window. Curls of grey smoke swirled from the cigarette Morgan had started smoking. Wheeler studied them.

She mudda di' bring her by dem. So wha if she in remember, in know dem as good as him?

Wheeler cut her eyes at Donelle: *Stupid head!*

Donelle said, "Uncl'Morgan, y'not turning on d'radio?"

Taking the cigarette from his mouth, Morgan reminded him, "It now Lent."

The Hillman danced over the bumps in the road. Wheeler watched Geraldine's broad back jiggling on the bench seat in front.

High above the Verdant table, heading out to the country, the black tar gave way to silky dirt, its surface baked pale and hard by the dry-season sun. They swept along the seasoned road towards the string of make-do villages: Reverie, Trenchant and Stout.

Half an hour later, entering Stout, Morgan bipped his horn, driving slower now. An old-timer sitting out on a shallow veranda tipped his hat in response.

Wheeler sat up. "Uncl'Morgan, dis whey y'from?"

"Not here." Donelle was quick to correct her.

"No, not this part." Morgan was looking at Wheeler in the rear-view mirror. "We jus taking a drive."

Wheeler knew only that her uncle had come from the country. She didn't know which part.

An ancient truck and a broken-down wooden bus had stood at the entrance to the village. The baked dirt road curled into the centre of Stout. More small unpainted houses. Wheeler wondered if anyone could stand up straight in them. There were children staring back at her, legs ashen, clothes torn. They took their fill of the Hillman… they took their fill of Wheeler and Donelle as the car crept by—

Slow, vengeful stares.

More children. More stares. As the children of Stout stared, she felt the force of their eyes press the air on the inside of the car.

"Uncl'Morgan, how dey looking?"

"Uncl'Morgan, why dey staring?" Donelle this time.

"Dey jus looking."

Further on, at a hairpin turn, the Hillman struggled and slowed down.

Wheeler swerved round. The children were still staring. Were still there. Her eyes landed on a small boy, younger than the others, standing alone in a yard. Wheeler extended her arm on an impulse and waved, like a queen in a carnival parade.

Donelle burst out laughing, slapping his knee and clapping his hands. "Dey goan put you in d'Crazy House!"

Wheeler yanked her arm back into the car as if scorched.

"Y-eh, d'Crazy House." Donelle nodded in satisfaction.

Let out of the car at the top of the Cut, Wheeler stared, unfocused, still shaken by the drive through Stout. Dem chil'ren *staring!* Donelle saying bout d'Crazy House. He di' make a pappy-show outa her!

Donelle walked downhill as Wheeler held back. She had fallen into a period of unhappy silence, gazing at the uncaring sky as mango trees and the tops of other trees hurried by, as Donelle chatted to their uncle on the way home.

He di' know more tings dan her. He even know whey Uncl'Morgan come from.

Wheeler's sense of embarrassment and despair grew. She remembered holding on to the winder earlier, head spinning from window to window, while Donelle sat back looking relaxed. She studied the back of Donelle's head in the failing light: his close-cropped hair, the orb-like outline of his head leading round to that troubled, ruffled forehead. Wheeler's sharp eyes darkened: *Stupid head!*

There were slicks of dark orange wherever she looked – on the water, the leaves of the trees, the tips of Donelle's ears. Stupid head or not, he seemed less backward than her. Full of knowledge she didn't have.

Nearing the house, first Donelle then Wheeler slowed down. There was someone shouting somewhere deep inside. She waited, trying to figure out what was happening. Like the spare single notes of a steelpan, the sounds kept breaking, the location of the noise kept on changing.

"Hesta!"

Wheeler's insides lurched upon hearing her sister's name. There it was again—

She flew past the terraced yard, propelled by the thrill of discovering what kind of trouble Hesta was in.

"Idle."

"*Stu*-pid..."

"Y'head *hard*?" Innez shouting.

They ran to the bottom entrance, making their way to where the noise led them – the kitchen.

"Ah-ah... All-you don't go down dere." Leaning out of her bedroom window, Celeste stopped them. Her voice was urgent and loud.

Donelle came to a quick halt. Wheeler struggled, not wanting to stop. She carried on, then turned back round.

Celeste's determined face hung down. "All-you go an sit out on d'steps. Don't go in dere."

Small sun-kissed clouds dotted the sky out to the harbour and to the far side of the headland. The colours of twilight dirtied the water. As evening began turning into night, soft silhouetted hilltops became one. The rush of excitement, the energetic surge brought on by Innez cussing out Hesta started dribbling away from Wheeler. She and Donelle remained out on the Cut as the row in the kitchen continued.

"Wha y'tink she do?"

Donelle shrugged from where he reclined two steps up.

Wheeler looked across the terraced yard, over to Celeste's bedroom; their aunt was still in there, the narrow door part-open. "Why Tant'Celeste don't go nowhere?" she asked. "Why she in never leave d'house?"

Donelle tipped forward. His eyes followed Wheeler's to the darkened doorway. "She in warnt Floyd t'trow she clothes in d'yard."

Wha?

Quick-fired birds crossed the sky, racing for home. A familiar feeling took hold of Wheeler, a stirring in her bowels. She gazed into Donelle's face. He had an amused look in his eyes.

"D'last time she go ta work, Floyd di' trow all she clothes out d'house."

"She used t' *work*?"

The smile fell from Donelle's face. He gestured. "Jus dere. Down in the lumberyard."

Wheeler's eyes dropped to the edge of the shore, to the toy-like complex of the lumberyard. There were planks of wood stacked to the edge of the deserted yard. She started blinking, moistening her eyes. The open forecourt extended down to the road. There was an L-shaped building to the side and the back, a bright red door...

How dey ant coulda bin part o' all dat?

Her eyes landed on Donelle.

How she could believe wha he say?

A deep frown divided Wheeler's brow. Still, she started reimagining who her aunt might be.

Tant'Celeste used t'work? She di' work down dere?

Donelle said, "Floyd in warnt her living here no more."

Wheeler looked to the veranda. She half-expected to see Floyd glaring down at them. "Wh-h..why yer mudda in stop him trowing she clothes out d'house?"

"She does let him do wha he warnt."

"Why he in warnt Tant'Celeste living here no more?"

A kind of calm had come over Donelle. "Ah in know."

A long truck took the turn on Wharf Road and Wheeler's thoughts travelled the turn with it, carrying what she'd learnt: She ant used t'work, Floyd di' chuck she clothes out d'house.

Reflecting on what Donelle already knew, Wheeler looked up at him. He seemed even mightier than before.

The row in the kitchen had ended. No sound of Innez's voice.

"Y'in coming?"

Wheeler waited. Donelle appeared content to stay right where he was. She set off alone in the pink twilight, the remainder of the dark sun glowing – a discarded chunk of charcoal hurled across the sky.

When she came home from school or church, Celeste was always there: hanging up clothes, taking them down, finishing off cooking or standing back against the counter, serving spoon in hand.

Christmas – carnival, she ant di' here all d'time! E'rybody else in town jumping up.

Wheeler glanced back, a sad, regretful look on her face. She moved on, fearing Celeste might look out of her window.

Her sisters were above in the kitchen.

Coming round the house, Wheeler tiptoed up the ramp. She leaned against the outdoor sink and peeped in through the kitchen window. She saw Adele and Hesta.

Dere in nobody else in dere.

Saturday afternoons, Adele and Hesta baked bread and buns under Innez's supervision. Coconut buns, nipple rolls and tin loaves. Weighing and sieving, mixing and kneading a hillside of dough. They crammed enough bread in the kerosene oven to carry the household part way through the week.

She in see nobody else.

Wheeler made her way to the open doorway, to the rumble of Hesta starting up complaining.

"Why she leave us on we own – *Who* she goan giv two lash?"

"Hush, na. Why y'in keep y'voice down?" cautioned Adele, eyes straying to the high ceiling.

"D'bread *bunning!*"

"It in bun—"

"It bunning. How d'*hell* ah know not t'open d'oven door?"

Adele placed her arms around Hesta, held her.

Having committed the ultimate crime in bread-making, Hesta appeared reluctant to be quelled. She shoved Adele away.

"Wha d'*hell*!"

Wheeler gawped at Hesta – *cussing*! – as her sister swung at a fly.

Adele's eyes landed on Wheeler. Wheeler stared right back, unflinching. Adele's face looked swollen with heat and sweat like Hesta's.

Why she should feel sorry f'dem? She in sorry f'dem: kiddy d'Hesta, kiddy d'Adele wid she hand on she waist.

Not forgetting why she'd come, Wheeler continued to meet Adele's gaze. "Donelle say Tant'Celeste don't never leave d'house. Because o' *Floyd*."

A ripple on Adele's tired face. Hesta stood still, no longer swatting. The blue kerosene burped in its upside-down bottle.

"Donelle need t'mind he biznis." Adele folded her arms and angled her head.

"She used ta work. Is true! Floyd trow she clothes out in d'yard!"

Her sisters shared a conspiratorial look—

"Tant'Celeste carnt leave di house cause o' Floyd."

"She does go out sometimes," Hesta muttered.

"Why all-you does *lie*?" Wheeler marvelled. She shook her disbelieving head: Adele, she face in a state. Hesta looking like... looking like she *still* warnta lie!

"Y'say... dat Floyd in hate her. Now y'saying she does leave d'house."

Adele lowered her arms and started coming forward.

"Show some res-*pek*! We yer big sisters. Who y'tink y'talking to?"

Wheeler jerked back. "Y'say… he in hate her. All-you does do wha all-you *warnt*… all-you does do wha*ever* all-you warnt – an lie. Does *always* lie!"

Hesta threw out a long arm.

Wheeler fled, bumping her side on the kitchen door. She clipped up the volcanic yard, not looking back and spun round at the top.

Hesta hadn't followed her. Neither sister had. Wheeler panted and squatted on the narrow gutter ledge at the back of the house. She hugged her knees. After looking around, she lowered her head and wept.

She wept over her mother: *Who dere now t'stick up f'her?* Over rough treatment from her sisters: *She coulnt trust dem. Dey does stand-up f'one anudda. Dey does do wha dey like.*

She cried as hard as she could for Celeste—

"Who crying out dere?"

Floyd!

Wheeler made for the bushes. Changing her mind, she clawed up the back wall.

Going down for her supper, she came to a decision.

She in *never* talking t'she sisters again.

Wheeler cut her eye on Hesta, lifting the heavy cocoa pot from the stove. Adele hadn't come into the kitchen yet. Wheeler cut her eye on her, too, in her mind.

Debris from the day's baking was thrown together on the counter, a different display from the usual. The kitchen smelled of wreckage, of days of hard chewing. Misshapen, salvaged, burnt, the loaves would still have to be eaten.

Hesta poured the cocoa, slouching from cocoa cup to cocoa cup.

Wheeler sat back.

She not talking t'dem - not like before, when she wasn't talking t'Donelle - she in *never* talking t'dem again.

Celeste stood to the side, sawing into a loaf of bread. Wheeler's mood softened. She tried to avoid looking at Celeste.

She coulnt ask a grown person dey biznis, she coulnt tell Tantie Celeste wha Donelle di' say.

She decided to forgive all the rough treatment she'd ever suffered from Celeste.

When Donelle came down, he glanced at Wheeler then looked away, perhaps regretting what he'd told her. Sensing his apparent regret, Wheeler sighed.

Donelle shoulnt blame heself.

She was in no doubt who was to blame.

Adele saying t'mind he biznis. Hesta saying bout dey ant does go out sometime. She was goan remember not t'talk t'dem, f'all d'*lies* dey does tell!

"We ready!" Hesta cried out.

Every morning when she wake up, she goan remember. When she get she food, she goan remember. She goan

203

remember when she going t'bed. She goan remember an *ignore* dem.

Her sisters came climbing the stairs, their voices crawling ahead of them. Wheeler sat up in bed, arms folded, poised to make good on her pledge.

She di' polish she church shoe so dey woulnt hav *nutting* t' tell her.

The soft leather church shoes had been left to the side of the open doorway, where her sisters might see them. Wheeler recalled what else Donelle had said, and agreed with him.

Is true, Tant'Innez in hav no control over Floyd. She di' hear she ant tell him, "Y'in hear me talking t'you?" But Floyd in lissening, he jus run out d'house. "Why ah ha' t'respek her?" she di' hear him say. He musta bin talking bout Tant'Celeste.

Wheeler pushed herself back up against the headrail, wondering what was happening.

She sisters di' taking dey time coming.

Adele walked in. Hesta followed.

"Wha she say?"

"Wha she could say?" Hesta answered. "Ah tell her ah di' smell d'bread bunning."

As if to say *Nah dis again*, Adele unbuttoned her bodice and slumped on the end of the bed.

Hesta flung off her housedress. Her lower half was clad

in a pair of light panties. Her long, black body appeared silken in the poor light. She pulled on her nightdress. "She say she telling we mudda." Hesta snorted. "M'mudda in sen me here t'bake no bread!"

Wheeler screwed up her face.

D-ey... dey dint self *notice* she ignoring dem!

The following day, before church, Wheeler let Adele do her hair. Adele loosened then replaited the three soft plaits – two at the back – then attached a green striped ribbon to the top plait.

As Wheeler set off to wait on the veranda, one of her sisters made a sound: "*Hg-h.*" She glanced back, hoping for trouble. She wanted to hear them say *Y'in saying thanks?* But Adele was just clearing her throat.

The next day Wheeler worked hard at serving up the silent treatment: saying nothing on the way to school, doing her homework by herself.

Even self she need help.

All the while Adele and Hesta seemed not to notice. They plaited Wheeler's hair, walked her to school, made sure she got home.

Two days in, Hesta said: "Y'tink y'smart?" She shook her head. "Y'too rude."

At last dey di' notice.

Ecstatic, Wheeler lifted her head from her reading book and looked around.

Adele sat at the end of the bed. Frowning, she examined Wheeler from under her eyes. "Y'kerrying on like y'in hav no manners."

Wheeler struggled not to lose her temper. Is d'two o' *dem* dat di' wrong, not her! Dey know wha Floyd do – *still* dey lying! Adele acting like she forget.

Wheeler swallowed hard, muttered, "Schu-pes."

31

It was in that final hour before the sun went down, when the distant chatter of seabirds and schoolyard children could be heard, when looking down from the height of the Cut, solid blue shapes could be seen at the shore, that Wheeler set off up the lane, determined to wreck the Girl Guide meeting.

Wasn't enough t'jus *ignore* dem!

The lengthening evening light exposed dents and scratches all around the Guide Hall walls. Lumps and scrapes and scratches, its builders' marks.

Wheeler marched on alone, dressed in her homeclothes, squinting at the bell tower rising above the Guide Hall. She had told Donelle what she was doing.

He di' go crazy wid he self! He dint warnt t'come.

As she descended the turn, the rustle of roadside trees replaced the murmur of the seafront. As she advanced on the Guide Hall door, the mutter of organised thinking – circles of girls seated mumbling – became all Wheeler heard.

Heads swinging as one, a set of them turned as Wheeler strode in. Bewildered eyes followed her. She experienced the icy cool shock of being the centre of attention. The naked scrutiny of the girls threatened to derail her. For a moment.

Wheeler rushed towards Hesta. She never made it—

"Eh-eh! Wha going on?"

The bellow of Miss Bench came between them. Adele hurled forward and grabbed Wheeler. "She come f'us. We ant warnt us t'go home!"

"*W-h-ho*?" the Guide Leader babbled.

"Ah come… Ah com-e—! To show all-you—"

Pulling her backwards, Adele steered Wheeler out of the hall.

Hesta kneeled up off the floor. She followed them like a trailing apology.

"Y'warnt Miss Bench t'tell? Y'warnt Innez t'beat you?" Adele slammed Wheeler against the outside of the building.

Wheeler's pupils spun. "All-you, all-you—"

"Wha d'hell she doing?" Hesta demanded.

Keeping her safe from Hesta, Adele shoved Wheeler off out to the lane. "Le' we get out from here."

Hesta said. "Cele-s… Celeste in sen her here."

Adele rolled her eyes. "Of *course* she in sen her here. *Nobody* in sen her here!"

"So wha d'*hell*—" Hesta sprang at Wheeler.

Adele grabbed hold of Hesta's arm. "Y'warnt Miss Bench t'hear you?"

Hesta's entire body heaved. She seemed to be trying, trying then failing to keep herself under control. "Y-ou!" She pointed. After peering down at Wheeler as on something defective, Hesta took off, arms flying.

Three turned to two, two turned to one, as Adele walked off up the lane. Wheeler stood on her own, unrepentant.

Adele di' drag her… All dem gyuls looking at her!

The evening rustled through the tall yellow trees. There was the sound of birds clawing and crackling in the fallen leaves. Wheeler stood still.

She di' nearly cause trouble in d'Guide Hall. She di' nearly put sheself in trouble.

A level look came into her eyes.

Adele was waiting for her at the top of the lane. "C'mon," she said.

Wheeler hesitated. Hesta di' try an hit her. She di' smell she sister stink breath.

She started walking towards Adele. She said, "Hesta di' try an tump me for no reason."

Adele moved on, seeming to arrive at her own assessment of what Hesta had done.

"She di' say Tant'Cel-es-te—"

"Don't take on Hesta!"

"But she say—"

"Y'in hear me? Y'tink we in doing we best f'you, hm-m? Dat wha y'tink?"

She dint know *wha* she tink.

"H-gh. Well, we doing we best. We not telling you tings f'yer own good."

The night brought with it the incessant insect brawl. An invisible outer world pressed against the house: buzzing, chiming, chirping. The full-throated croaks of bullfrogs. The shapes of the sisters' belongings crouched and bunched in the dim light of the room.

Alone in the bedroom, Wheeler changed into her nightdress, short chin emerging around the neck.

The silent treatment was over. Walking down from the Guide Hall, Wheeler realised she was talking again. "We mudda in say when she sending f'us?" she'd asked Adele.

Suspicion now hung over everything they'd done and said, mistrust of her sisters having blossomed in recent days.

"She in say?" Wheeler softened her voice, hoping to coax something out of Adele. "Why all-you in tell me?"

At the bottom of the spur, Adele had finally answered. "She in say when she sending f'us."

Wheeler scowled.

She in know wedda or not she believe wha she sister say.

There was laughter coming from the other side of the house: Jonathan. Followed by the sound of Adele's voice: "Evening."

Wheeler headed out.

As she made her way past the sitting room, she caught

the sense of people walking in the dark. From the safe harbour of the veranda, she stared out. The night was animated and buoyant. A sound-wall surrounded the house. Fireflies appeared to sink into the dense chorus as if it were the night's very material.

The walkers had stopped. She couldn't make anyone out.

"All-you going by d'Villa?" Adele asked.

"We going all d'way t'Verdan'!" one of them cried. Everybody laughed: Adele and Jonathan on the veranda steps, the people out on the Cut. Wheeler strained forward, still trying to decide who was who.

"Say evening t'y'ant f'me," one of them said.

"Aw-right!" Adele cried back.

As the walkers carried on, Wheeler wondered which aunt.

32

Y'tink we in doing we best f'you… Dat wha y'tink? We not telling you tings f'yer own good.

As she stood at the concrete sink, Adele's words returned to Wheeler's mind. She stopped scrubbing and looked in on Innez and Celeste. It had taken a week for her to look at Celeste straight. She stared at her now.

The two aunts stood a fraught distance apart to the side of the kitchen counter, discussing the day's messages – discussing money.

Wheeler's fingers curled.

She di' fraid Tant'Innez. She di' like keeping outa she way.

In her shabby housedress, Celeste drew herself to her full height and looked down on Innez, a look that seemed to say she had no intention of disguising the disdain she felt. Innez flicked notes and coins onto the counter.

Wheeler looked up after one of the dropped coins hit a metal cup. She caught the look on Innez's face.

Tant'Innez di' look sick. Was not d'first time she di' see she ant look sick wid sheself, when she face Tant'Celeste.

Dressed in her crisp work tunic, Innez seemed to have no answer to Celeste's snub. She laid down a final coin. A nervous look came into Wheeler's face.

Sometimes coming back home f'she lunch Tant'Innez di' look mash up when she face Tant'Celeste. Even tho she does do up she hair nice an keep sheself nicer'n Tant'Celeste.

Wheeler lowered her head, not wanting to be caught looking.

"Dem chil'ren, dem chil'ren know whey dey going? Dey better not *waste* dis mon-eey!"

Wheeler grew worried for Celeste.

Was Tant'Celeste who sen Adele an dem t'buy messages. Be Tant'Celeste fault if d'money waste.

Innez came out into the yard. Seeing the look of hatred as she glared back at Celeste, a pained expression appeared on Wheeler's face: wasn't jus *Floyd* who di' hate Tant'Celeste.

Later, when she saw Celeste shucking at the juking board, Wheeler's heart saddened.

Tant'Innez in *care* wha happen t'Tant'Celeste. She in *care* bout all d'trouble Floyd di' make her see!

Staring down from the veranda in the bleak afternoon heat, Wheeler pictured what Floyd had done: dresses and skirts lay tossed from the bedroom doorway, a single shoe flung further out near the Cut. Outside Celeste's bedroom, shrivelled and darned panties and brassieres clung to a tangled shrub. Private things Wheeler had only ever seen shoved to the end of the washing line. She imagined Floyd hurling Celeste's old house clothes next.

He di' fling *every*ting? Or jus *slam* everyting on the ground?

Wheeler's eyes landed on the cracked concrete path pointing away from the house. A hot breeze sent clawlike shadows scratching along the broken ground.

Dat's wha he di' do. He di' *slam* dem.

And Wheeler pictured Floyd tearing back into the house.

He di' go back f'any little stray ting he di' drop.

She clenched her teeth.

How he could do she ant ting like dat? He di' slam down Tant'Celeste tings right *dere*, jus like—

Celeste appeared below, wearing a pale housedress. Wheeler crouched down behind the veranda wall. After shaking out a long, wayward floor mat by the Cut, Celeste placed a palm to the centre of her back. She searched around, eyes skittish and anxious. Spying through the fretwork in the wall, Wheeler imagined her aunt not as she was now, but in a skirt and blouse on her way back from work, climbing the Cut then slowing down.

Celeste folded the mat and strolled back into the house.

He di' stand up here an watch? Floyd musta make Tant'Celeste fraid o' leaving d'house after dat.

Wheeler eased onto her feet. Her questioning eyes

roamed the darkened doorway leading to Floyd's bedroom. Standing out on the veranda, she had the sense of being exposed like Celeste's clothes. She slunk off to the back of the house.

33

The next morning, dressed in her church clothes, Wheeler ran down the veranda steps, jockeying between Donelle and Jonathan. Hesta and Adele appeared below, leaving by the lower entrance. The younger group became the frontrunners after elbowing and pushing through the older girls. Targeting Jonathan, Hesta threw out her right arm but missed him. He nearly lost a shoe.

Taking their time, the sisters drifted down, everyone crisp-looking in their Sunday clothes. Wheeler was wearing the new church dress, which Hesta had collected from the seamstress. It had been sewn from the striped material Adele had bought in town.

Still aggrieved, Wheeler glanced back.

How dey mean dey doing dey best f'her?

Russell Street ran quiet. There were adults and a few children stretched ahead in the soundless heat. The stillness of the morning was brittle and ear-numbing. Gone was the church service seeping around windows and open doors. In the solemn, quiet weeks of Lent, the absence of the radio followed Wheeler and the others along the road.

Going by the cinema gate, Wheeler gazed down at the water: an impossible shade of blue. The corner of the bay rocked as if something heavy had taken off nearby or further out. She turned to Donelle, the veins in his temples grumpy and swollen.

After he di' say he hear d'woman in Floyd bedroom, Floyd di' keep he radio up loud in dere. He di' start coming back home late Saturday evening, since Lent.

Catching Wheeler's eye, Donelle grunted, "Wha?"

She pretended to be looking elsewhere: at the row of little houses on the far side of the road. At her sisters.

Dey di' getting fardah behind.

Adele and Hesta disappeared at the turn in the road. Wheeler strode on with Donelle and Jonathan.

Not a single motorbike or car on the road. All three glanced down as they arrived at the Cable & Wireless junction.

Emerging from the sleepiness of Sunday school, Wheeler drifted across the elementary schoolyard. She turned her head, not yet ready to take on the full brunt of the sun. Reaching the other side, she leaned against the retaining wall, blinking. The churchyard was deep below her, part in sunlight, the heated slope of the church roof right in front of her, seeming close enough for Wheeler to reach over and touch.

The church organ was still seesawing, the congregation

still singing. Easing down off her tiptoes, she turned her back to the church.

Hesta di' go f'she choir practice. She di' go tree times, since Miss Hughes di' ask her. But she in go no more.

Wheeler gazed back to the school entrance, where a dozen children stood waiting at a standpipe for a drink, Donelle amongst them. Sunday school had finished early.

Miss Agnes di' jus *stop*. Di' say dey could go.

The congregation started powering down. Wheeler twisted towards the churchyard. A final gaudy flourish from the organ, twiddles and all. In the stark silence that followed, she once again started worrying about her aunt.

Did Tant'Celeste used t'go t'church? She in tink she remember seeing her. Whey else she used t'go? She used t'go t'sou-sou, like Tant'Innez does do?

The congregation still hadn't started coming out. Older girls stood chatting in the distance, between the standpipe and the lavatory block. Other kids Wheeler's age ran around the sky-high schoolyard kicking up dust.

Tant'Celeste does do d'cooking, does kill d'chicken, does do everyting. Why Floyd in warnt dey ant in d'house?

People started shuffling out from church. Their voices scurried up the church wall like escaping birds. Wheeler glanced down. Straw hats and veils, starched shirts and ties. Young bodies, old ones. The flicker of ivory fans.

"Y'in coming?"

Jonathan stood waiting. He gestured to Wheeler to come on.

Why Floyd in warnt Tant'Celeste in d'house?

Wheeler started running. There was only one way to find out.

After lunch, with the countertop streaked and drying, with everyone else gone elsewhere, Wheeler headed back down to talk to Celeste.

She hav t'catch her fore she disappear in she room.

Celeste sat sideways to the kitchen counter.

Wheeler's feet stuttered. They refused to cooperate, despite what she'd decided to do.

Wasn't right to ask grown people dey biznis. Y'should go up an behave yeself. Tant'Celeste'll fling y'down like one o' dem chickens in d'yard, her reluctant feet seemed to be saying.

Resisting the impulse to behave and go away, Wheeler continued down the stairs. Celeste looked round. Wheeler pressed herself into the wall.

"You an Donelle fall out?"

Wheeler shook her head and cut across to the front counter, where Celeste sat eating. "He say Floyd trow yer clothes out d'house, when you bin t'work."

Celeste did not blink. She continued chewing the food in her mouth, did not alter the rhythm of her chewing. She fixed her eyes to a place across the water.

Dint say don't put yer mout whey it don't belong. Tant'Celeste dint fling her down.

Wheeler became unstable on her feet. It was a sensation like sinking.

A look of exhaustion appeared in Celeste's yellowed eyes as she stopped chewing and started swallowing. "Come." She pushed the plate of food aside. "Come."

Wheeler followed as Celeste led the way, past the silent oven and the open doorway, past the shower and lavatory cubicles under the stairs. Her aunt glanced back from her bedroom door as if checking to see if Wheeler was still there.

She was still there.

The dark room beckoned. It was a place Wheeler had never expected to enter, a forgotten-about place. A room she had looked into from the other side of the house, a place she'd avoided approaching even when she had called out for Celeste's help.

An Tant'Celeste dint come out.

Wheeler peered in from the passageway. The room was dim, even by the dull standards of the ground floor. The shadow of the afternoon sun fell through the open windows. Stepping closer, hesitant, Wheeler raked her eyes around the room, corner to corner, wall to wall: a bedside cupboard, the usual brass bed, a tall chest of drawers, a dark wood wardrobe taking up space.

D'same old-people tings she di' see in Tant'Innez bedroom.

The door to the terraced yard was shut. Wheeler hovered.

Sitting on the edge of the bed, Celeste dipped forward and felt behind the bedside cupboard. She pulled a crumpled paper bag into the open and reached into it.

Wheeler went and sat beside her aunt.

Celeste removed small items of clothing from the bag: bootees, a pair of frilly panties. Next she pulled out a small cream-coloured dress. She held it up with her long thin arms. "Dey dint tink she would live."

A perplexed look appeared on Wheeler's face. Her eyes grew large.

"We had t'baptise her *quick*."

Wheeler reached out and held the tiny crocheted dress, sensing that Celeste wanted her to. The frilly panties sat between her and her aunt. From inside the paper bag Celeste removed a sheet of paper that looked to have been ripped into little pieces then stuck back together with Sellotape. When Wheeler looked at her, Celeste appeared helpless.

'Sif she coulnt hole up sheself. She in tink she ant could look like dat.

Wheeler laid down the dress.

Celeste held out the bumpy piece of paper, hands shaking. Wheeler read it: "Certifi-ca-tion of birth," she said. Celeste nodded. Wheeler then said the words "Edith Michelle". There was a look of regret on Celeste's face.

'Sif she di' sorry f'everyting bad she di' do, everyting she di' say.

Wheeler lowered her eyes. She traced the mends on the birth certificate.

Meanwhile, Celeste folded up the baptismal dress. She returned it to the paper bag with the booties and panties. Wheeler handed Celeste the birth certificate. "Floyd," was all Celeste said.

"Why he trow yer clothes in d'yard?"

Celeste stood up and walked with the bag to the other side of the room, as if searching for somewhere new. Wheeler's body swerved round.

She in call her fast. She in answer neida.

Wheeler's eyes followed Celeste around the room.

She di' come an ask she ant sumting, but she di' find out sumting else. Tant'Celeste di' call she dead baby Edith Michelle.

At the top of the bed Celeste removed the pillows. She lifted the striped mattress. Clumps of coconut husk hung out of it. She shoved the paper bag inside the ruptured mattress, tidied it up.

"Tant'Celeste, why Floyd in warnt you in d'house?"

Arranging the pillows on top of the mattress, Celeste answered, "Don't worry yerself, chile, do."

On leaving the room, a shadow appeared overhead. Floyd was descending the kitchen stairs. Wheeler watched him stop.

ANNE HAWK

He di' chuck she ant clothes in d'yard. He di' tear up she baby paper... But Tant'Celeste di' stick it back. Tant'Celeste di' come back!

Floyd glared down. The look in his eyes was incendiary. He said, "Y'tink ah done? Ah in finish wid you."

Wheeler looked round. Celeste stood in the bedroom doorway behind her. It was a threat that could have applied to either of them.

34

Stewfish and broth for lunch; cocoa tea, saltfish souse and bakes later on; a slice of coconut bun in the afternoon when they came home from school.

Strolling past the sitting room, crumbs on his shirt and around his mouth, Donelle appeared to be uninterested in what Wheeler was saying. A pool of water reflected on the ceiling. The dry, salty scent of seawater filled the room.

Again, she told Donelle about Celeste's bedroom: the taped-together piece of paper. About going in Celeste's bedroom in the first place! The details tumbled out of her.

"She hav a tiny baby dress. And a tear-up piece o' paper wid she baby name. It say *Edith Michelle.*"

At the doorway Donelle broke away. He swiped the coconut crumbs from his mouth and strolled to the far end of the veranda. Coming alongside him, Wheeler reached up to the rough concrete ledge. She puzzled over what he might be thinking and followed his gaze out across the view. There was a small tugboat at the entrance of the bay, chugging water, waiting to escort an unseen ship to the port. Although she wanted to, Wheeler did not mention her mother. Instead, she studied the look on Donelle's face.

He lips di' close. He look like he chewing – he in still chewing!

She wondered what might be wrong. She thought she knew.

He dint hav nobody who di' die. She an Tant'Celeste di' diffrent. Dey di' know bout people leaving an not coming back. Donelle? He in care bout *nobody* but heself!

Donelle continued to stare. There was something angry bubbling in his eyes now. Wheeler looked away.

He in still stewing over wha Floyd di' do him?

The evening before, Floyd had threatened to cut off Donelle's ears. Wheeler had heard the squeaky whimpering as she walked out of her room. It was coming from the veranda.

Donelle was out there, seated on a chair. Floyd was standing behind him, shirt off, a large pair of scissors in his hand. He was supposed to be trimming Donelle's hair.

Snip, snip, snip!

Floyd had waved the tailor's scissors in a circle above his brother's head. "Y'warnt ah cut off yer ears!"

"Ah in warnt y'cut meh ears off!" Donelle had squealed, pleading. It seemed that the higher he shriek, the louder the pair of scissors snipped.

"Y'in warnt ah cut yer ears off – well sit still den!"

How Donelle goan siddown still wid Floyd snapping he scissors round he head?

Wheeler had remained on the landing, watching.

She di' feel sorry f'Donelle den. She could feel sorry f'Celeste too. How he carnt feel d'same?

Wheeler shook her head.

He di' only feel sorry f'heself. She jus goan *leave*!

As she approached the veranda steps, Wheeler looked back. "Y'not coming by d'lane?"

Donelle shook his head, mumbled, "Ah can go later."

Walking back, Wheeler asked him, "He in cut you?"

From the depths of his misery, Donelle gave Wheeler a pained look.

She said, "Floyd does like troubling udda people. He di' trouble Tant'Celeste."

To this Donelle nodded, then returned to staring off towards the docks.

"*Dat's* why he di' tear up Tant'Celeste paper an try an *trow* her out! He say he goan do something more, too."

"How y'mean?"

"Ah in know."

35

A late chicken uproar – a different one from the cackling at dawn.

Heading back from sweeping the yard, dragging the yard broom behind her, Wheeler slowed down at the front of the house. A sheet of brown feathers fantailed up ahead. Blood-strewn cackles reached her ears. As she came clear of the house, the skirt of Celeste's housedress billowed out.

There was dumb astonishment on Celeste's face as she swirled around. She was clinging to a headless chicken, its legs pumping. Blood drained down her arm, a trail of it pointing to where the dance had started: the chopping stump to the side of the door. The frenzied fleeing of the chicken was mapped in streaks of blood on the ground.

Staring up at the yard, Wheeler's lips trembled at the sight of the Saturday kill gone wrong; at the rosette of blood round the neck of the tormented bird. Mouth open, her eyes followed Celeste up the side of the rocky slope, where her aunt next spun round, where the chicken next led her. Blood on her clothes, on her throat, as Celeste came to a halt.

"Tant'Celeste, come wash y'face!" At the concrete sink, Hesta seemed to respond in slow time. She pushed her washing aside.

The pumping chicken slumped limp in Celeste's hand. The cackling rumpus continued from other hens inside the bushes.

Celeste lowered the butchered bird onto the wooden kitchen stump. Eyes vacant, she wandered into the house.

Forgetting she held it, Wheeler watched the yard broom drop to the ground.

Donelle came running from above. "Wha happen?"

"D'damn chicken break way when Celeste kill it. Y'in hear d'rest o' dem cackling?" Hesta asked.

"How come?" Donelle wanted to know. "H-how…?"

The shaft of the yard broom laid upside down.

Wheeler recalled what she'd seen: Tant'Celeste, an blood – an d'chicken. Before it di' die, she di' see d'chicken dragging she ant round d'yard.

Wheeler lifted her eyes to the slope.

She di' see headless chicken prance about. But she in see nutting like dat before.

36

They'd eaten the chicken the following day without wincing, with rice-n-peas and a slice of fried plaintain. One of the fleeing feet turned up on Donelle's plate. The neck was served on Wheeler's plate in rich gravy. And she'd mixed the bony meat together with the plaintain and rice-n-peas, not possessing the luxury of not eating it.

Towards the end of March, the first of the Easter kites appeared. A large fix-framed kite rising above the lumberyard from where it had been obscured by the branch of a coconut tree. A mystery kite set free from a surrounding hill. The kite's colours were green and orange.

"All-you come see!"

Summoned by Jonathan, Donelle then Wheeler ran out. They started walking backwards, following Jonathan's gaze.

Quieter than carnival, kite season started in the final waning week of Lent and culminated in a mass display on Easter Sunday. It signalled an end to the silencing of the steelbands and the radio, an end to the solemnity of Lent.

Jonathan started running from the edge of the terraced

yard. They chased after him. There was always one rogue Easter flyer unable to wait until the end of Lent. Here was this year's mystery kite.

Wheeler swivelled, eyes aimed skywards. "Whey it come from?" She chased Jonathan and Donelle further uphill.

Made using bamboo splint, coloured paper and twine, cloth tails of varying lengths were used to balance the ducking, twisting, lightweight kites.

The early kite strolled towards the breathless nothing above the bay. The strands of its long cotton tail floated across the face of the Anglican clock, time-defying.

"Whey it come from?" Wheeler smiled a fascinated, open smile.

Jonathan squinted, concentrating. "Out by Cem'try Hill."

Quarter of a mile up, the mystery kite angled south, riding an invisible current.

"Bw-oy, kite season come f'true, *oui*!"

A cryptic smile from Jonathan as Donelle spoke. "It not come yet," he promised, "but tings goan start happ'ning soon."

A few days after watching the rogue Easter kite, Wheeler spotted Jonathan and Donelle out on the veranda standing close together.

Is wha dey doing...? Wha dey saying? she wondered, walking out to join them.

Jonathan halted her with a look. He kept on talking, but

230

not before checking all around as if waiting to see who else might come out.

And Wheeler checked too.

Dere'n nobody coming.

Wha all-you doing? she'd intended to say. Instead she kept quiet and listened.

The brothers continued their exchange. Donelle was listing off a set of names.

"Who he?"

"H-e… he in m'class too."

Jonathan nodded. A slight jingle of marbles or coins in his pants pocket. "Okay. Tell dem bring dey money."

"How much all-you selling dem?"

Jonathan gave Donelle a price, adding: "Ah go bring dey kite on *Wen*sday. Y'un'erstand – Wensday. An not jus tell e'rybody."

Donelle nodded. "Ah un'erstand." Taken into his brother's confidence, a hint of pride replaced his usual downbeat expression.

Wheeler butted in. A competitive urge had overtaken her initial instinct to say nothing. "Ah know how y'make kite too."

Jonathan lifted an eyebrow.

She did not back down.

"Y'make kite wid bamboo. Y'turn d'string round and round and round. Y'stick it wid paper. An tie y'twine on top."

"Who teach y'dat?"

Who teach her? "Nobody."

"Hm-m." Jonathan shook his head. "All-you can come down Sat'day," he said, leaving. "Ah go help all-you make a kite."

Afterwards Wheeler asked, "Whey we mus go?"

"Down by Bounce," was Donelle's response.

37

When they came back from school on Friday, Donelle and Wheeler found Celeste waiting for them by the concrete sink.

"Geraldine come say she an Morgan going in d'country. Dey leaving now, if y'all warn t'come."

They gazed at one another. Wheeler and Donelle flew past Celeste, flung their books in the kitchen, bumped, staggered apart, and fought their way up the slope.

At the top wall, Wheeler darted off to the Cut. Donelle followed. He overtook her. Climbing the Cut, Wheeler panicked. She felt she was travelling backwards. The narrow steps seemed to be working against her. She took two, three of the steps together. The cousins' sparkling school shirts aligned midway up. At the top, Donelle and Wheeler exploded together onto the lane.

But Morgan had already gone. There was no sign of the car.

"Dey gone." Donelle pulled up, bent double, panting. Wheeler kept going.

"All-you coming?" Geraldine raised her arm, hailing

Wheeler from outside the iron gate. Idling under the crest of the lane, the grey Hillman waited for their aunt to get in.

"We com-*ing!*"

Geraldine opened the rear door. "All-you awright?"

Wheeler rolled onto the back seat. "Ye-s, Tant'Geldine. We awright."

Donelle pelted downhill, skidded as he neared the car. "Aft'noon, Uncl'Morgan." He jumped in the other side.

Out on the back lane three women walked abreast across the centre of the road. Morgan tut-tutted the horn, slowing down. Two of the women moved to the side of the road and walked on. Morgan stopped as the one at the back peered in on the driver's side.

"All-you going f'a drive?"

Morgan nodded.

She took a good look, prying around the inside of the car. "Oh-ho… Enjoy all-you drive."

Leaning across the bench seat, Geraldine thanked her. The other two women raised their hands as the car drove by.

Fighting the urge to kneel up and look back, Wheeler stared at the side of Morgan's neck. The car sped towards the roundabout. A circle of trees appeared to their left, a string of large houses to their right. The Guide Hall and its surrounding wall sped away in the rear-view mirror.

Resting his arm on the open window, Donelle said, "Whey y'going, Uncl'Morgan?"

Geraldine: "Celeste in tell all-you?"

Morgan answered, "We going in Mildenhall."

"Whey Morgan from," Geraldine said to Wheeler.

They took the first right at the roundabout, instead of carrying on up as before on the way to Stout.

Wheeler gazed out. More relaxed than her first time in the car, still one or two things returned to her mind, causing her to worry: Donelle asking their uncle to turn on the radio…

Like he di' ask Uncl'Morgan time an time before. She decided.

Donelle answering, "Not here!" when she di' ask, "Dis whey y'from?" – before self Uncl'Morgan di hav d'chance t'answer.

She pressed her head against the back seat. It seemed to Wheeler that her aunt and uncle belonged to Donelle more than they did to her.

They arrived at the steep mountain road then started sinking towards the Verdant basin. Grey harbour buildings appeared to the right. Tracts of green land and red-roofed houses fanned towards the shore. The Hillman crawled down the hillside road, curtseying and rotating at the turns. Geraldine leaned across the passenger seat and gazed down.

Wheeler scrutinised the couple.

Tant'Geldine di' hav she hair in a "do". She di' comb out she roller bumps. She di' see her in dat hairstyle before.

The car switched back then out. Morgan took a cigarette from his shirt pocket. He steered the car with one hand.

She di' see him do dat before.

With his other hand he sparked a match against the dashboard, held it up and lit the cigarette in his mouth.

Dat too.

She was getting to know them. Wheeler watched as the match took hold, as the cigarette's red light signalled and Morgan tossed the spent matchstick out of the window. Little knowing that, before reaching Mildenhall, she would no longer think of her aunt and uncle as near-strangers, Wheeler turned her attention to the view.

In Verdant the Hillman broke loose, sweeping off over the flat: past the Ventura Cinema and the Botanical Gardens. Ahead, weighty breadfruit trees lined the road. Large family-sized houses crouched in the sweet relief of the breadfruit shade. A line of schoolchildren strode from a wood-sided bus at the side of the road.

The silver-grey Hillman left the smooth black tar behind half a mile on, and climbed the rugged truck route taking them out of the capital. The car jumped and bumped, labouring along the unpaved road. Pockmarked and dusty, the truck route climbed through rich agricultural lands. Here they passed lines of field workers and country children along the side of the road.

With the dust rising, Morgan slowed down. Wheeler sagged low on the back seat, wary of hateful, hungry eyes. But the children here seldom looked into the car, occupied with getting home.

By late afternoon, the Hillman approached the windswept region of Mildenhall. On the way they'd seen a man leading a goat away from the centre of the road. They'd seen the broken body of an Easter kite, stretched and mangled along a power line. Donelle and Wheeler had pointed to the kite at the same time. Frayed pieces of cotton were all that was left of the tail. Relic of a past kite season, the bleached bamboo frame was as colourless as bone.

"Tant'Geldine?"

"H-hm?"

"Tantie Celeste daughter dead a long time?"

Geraldine nodded. "A long time."

Turning her face to the open window, Wheeler repeated the name Edith Michelle. "She still going on missing her, tho."

Geraldine nodded once more. "Big people does hav all kinda trouble in dey life. An not forget."

Keeping his eyes on the road, Morgan appeared to acknowledge what his wife had said. Without warning, Wheeler warmed to them. She'd caught the tilt of Morgan's head, a motion as faint as the falling of a strand of hair. With one tilt she'd had a glimpse into her aunt and uncle's lives, without knowing what she'd seen.

As they broke over one last hill, the full force of the south-easterly breeze hit the car. They descended towards the sugar fields: glistening acres of sweetness stretching as far as she could see. Before long they were sealed in on both sides by tall sugar cane. No sky. Just an endless rushing sound from the swishing, swaying stalks. A hissing current carried them as they drove along the sugar road.

Wheeler held on to the window winder and stared up, eyes transfixed by the elegant stalks, ears saturated with the noise. She had never experienced anything like this before.

"We dere," announced Donelle.

Leaning closer to Morgan, Wheeler whispered, "Uncl'Morgan, we dere?"

He turned to her. "We dere." Then he started slowing down.

The wall of sugar cane ruptured to the left side of the car. The whitewashed walls of the old sugar mill stood back from the road. A seam of little dwellings appeared to the right of it.

She di' looking forward to meeting Uncl'Morgan family.

The Hillman rolled up to a two-storey house on the left-hand side of the road. Its doors were wide open. There were metal signs nailed on the side and front of the shop: pictures of beer bottles, soapboxes, rusting cigarette packets. Morgan pulled into the pump yard on the far side of the shop. Rolling out from the back seat, Donelle ran ahead of him then waited at the door.

There was a dirt track leading away from the yard, a handful of low wooden houses visible inside the trees.

Climbing out of the car, lurching to her right, Wheeler asked, "We not going by Uncl'Morgan an dem house?"

Geraldine eased out. "Morgan in hav no family left in dere." She shut the passenger door.

The stock of the shop dangled from the ceiling, stood in the corners or else lined the walls – buckets, coal pots, chicken wire, fishing poles; with foodstuffs arranged on shelves behind a darkwood counter. Stopping serving as they walked in, the woman behind the counter hailed Morgan and Geraldine, pointed to Wheeler and Donelle. "Come. Get two drink."

The cousins went and stood at the shop counter while Morgan and Geraldine talked to people at a table looking onto the road.

Sipping her drink, Wheeler drifted towards a narrow exit where the canefields came close to the door, drawing her and sending in a breeze. The playful swaying, the low hissing of the stalks was reminiscent of her journey in the car.

"Mind y'in run into a snake!" someone called from inside the shop. And Wheeler stopped. She abandoned running into the tempting field.

They descended the Cut alongside one another in the deepening dusk. Placing one careful foot in front of another, Wheeler mumbled, "Dey di' hav everyting in dere." She bumped against Donelle. "Dey hav everyting jus standing round," she repeated, having said something similar before.

Pale-crested terns, short-tailed swifts crossed into the trees below.

Donelle looked up. Swift fruit bats criss-crossed overhead with tiny squeaks and snipes, tearing out to meet the night. They flew first in one direction then the next, wings folding and unfolding, whirling back and forth like dark rumours.

38

The following afternoon, Wheeler and Donelle set off to meet Jonathan. They took a narrow track veering away from the Cut. The noise of overheated crickets whizzed past as the cousins sped over the rock-hard dirt. Low weatherboard houses flew by, with front verandas and wide jaunty steps jutting out at various heights.

Since the first mystery kite, they had seen no other flying kites. With Easter just over a week away, bright bamboo kites had started appearing for sale in side yards and on front verandas.

Coming to a clearing, they slowed down. A brown weatherboard house reared out as the slope turned, its paintwork flaking and cracked. A fretted window snooped from beneath its triangular roof: Bounce's family home.

Jonathan sat bare-chested on a ledge to the side of the chattel house, surrounded by long bamboo canes. Bounce leaned out from the back of the house. Straight away he was into them. "H-gh, all-you come? *Wha...* t'make trouble?" He glowered. "Ah in know *why* ah should let all-you up in meh yard!"

The cluttered yard was strewn with the detritus of Bounce's family life: a little coal stove in the shade; a stack of Coca-Cola crates with empty bottles someone was collecting; a grey washtub, midway up, beside a battered enamel pail; further on, a raised water tank inside the trees at the top.

Hesitating at first, Wheeler climbed the wooden steps up to Bounce's yard.

Floyd di' cause trouble wid Bounce – not dem.

She turned to Donelle; his anxious eyes were still focused on Bounce.

A swerving clothesline ran the length of the slope. It ended near to where Jonathan was sitting. Wheeler ducked under the line and scooped down next to him. Jonathan smothered a giggle. "We soon start," he said.

Donelle came and sat on the ground beside them. A string of skeletal kite frames hung above their heads.

"Ah goan get all-you kite cut next," Jonathan said.

Bounce had strolled past them, gone to sit on a wooden stump further down.

Wheeler looked around. Her eyes returned to Jonathan. Everything seemed to be going so much slower than she'd expected. She sighed as Jonathan sized and cut the long bamboo strips, measuring one cane against another. Studying this painstaking approach, watching Bounce string together a frame from the strips Jonathan had been cutting, Wheeler grew less certain of her declared method of kite-making. She fell back, waiting for Jonathan to get round to her and Donelle.

Donelle sat with his knees bent staring at the shore opposite. Saturday afternoon, everywhere closed. The lumberyard forecourt stood vacant. Two squat figures stood out in the road.

Jonathan reached out, threw Bounce something. Wheeler stared then looked away, having lost the thread of what they were doing.

Bounce started talking: "H-uh. Floyd mad as hell. Jealous of a dead baby. Mad as hell, y'know?"

Wheeler's eyes darted towards Bounce.

"He mad f'so!"

She looked up at Jonathan.

"A baby. Yer ant an she sister wid d'same man." Bounce turned his head around to face Wheeler and Donelle. He nodded for emphasis. "*Floyd*! Floyd find out he *farda* di' giv d'dead baby he name. Man giv he name to d'dead *chile* and in he giv Floyd nutting!"

Wheeler looked to Jonathan for an explanation: Wha Bounce saying?

A wry light shone in Jonathan's eyes. He looked up but did not speak. His younger brother and cousin turned to one another.

Sumting di' happen... di' happen.

Something neither set of misted-over eyes seemed able to identify. Able to name.

This time Bounce focused his scandalous eyes on Donelle alone. "Yer ant and yer mudda wid d'same man!"

Nothing.

"She sister dey wid d'man. And *still* yer mudda wont leave d'man alone!"

Now Donelle pulled away.

"D'same man." Wheeler repeated the words. They meant nothing.

"H-gh. When Floyd find out, he try an kick yer ant out d'house, *oui*!" Bounce joked to himself as he kept on manoeuvring the frame.

Ma-co! Floyd di' call Bounce a maco. She know wha *dat* mean.

Wheeler looked again at Jonathan. He gave her an uneasy look.

The crickets had abandoned their quarrels by the time Donelle and Wheeler wandered back. Late afternoon light smothered them in gentle hues, as though warm and willing sunlight might somehow reverse time, might erase what they'd just heard.

They'd left their unfinished kites behind with Jonathan. He'd shown them how to bind the middle cross together and how to bind two more. Jonathan had shown them how to string the frame – had made the fish-mouth arc himself. Watching him twirl then curve the slim bamboo strips, Wheeler had cast aside her earlier spark of inspiration, had become sold on his method of kite-making instead.

"Who Floyd farda?" she asked, the slow, even rise of her chest echoing Donelle's. They knew something terrible had happened. But what?

Donelle shook his head. "Ah in know. He farda in Trin'dad or someplace."

Seeing the bewilderment on Donelle's face, Wheeler looked away.

Floyd di 'miss out on sumting. He di' blame dey ant. He di' try an chuck her out d'house.

Searching around, Jonathan had told them, "We in hav 'nough paper – ah go bring all-you kite f'all-you. We run out."

Tall, pinkish plumes stood to the side of the lumpen track. They nodded now and then as Donelle and Wheeler trundled by.

Wheeler recalled the stuck-together paper Celeste had shown her, the feel of it: both bumpy and smooth.

"He hav d'same farda as Edith Michelle?"

"Who?" Donelle's head swung up. He appeared to be thinking about many things. "Ah only know bout meh own farda."

She di' feel bad f'Donelle. F'd'way Bounce di' treat him.

And still yer mudda wont leave d'man alone. Still wont leave d'man…

"Why all-you in jus go an *live* wid all-you farda?"

Donelle didn't respond.

245

"All-you does go an see him."

"We does go an ask him f'money is all." He kept his eyes down.

They approached the Cut. As they trawled past the weatherboard houses, Christopher and his brother called down to them. One of the boys lifted an arm and Donelle waved back.

Wheeler and Donelle carried on, leaving the younger children behind.

39

A struggle between light and dark over the coming days. Tall white clouds blew in off the sea, startling and bright, blighting the once seamless skies. Clouds, massive and white, rising on the sea breeze, darkening the sun but still not lessening the heat.

"All-you hav sumting t'eat?"

"Yes, Tant'Geldine." A trickle of sweat down the side of Donelle's face.

"Come help me shell two groundnut."

Wheeler and Donelle stared at Geraldine from the lane, from behind the gate's iron grille. Geraldine sat at the top of her long kitchen steps. The cousins went up and joined her. She had a pail of groundnut shells at her elbow and a wide enamel basin in her lap.

"All-you okay?"

"We okay."

"All-you can eat all d'groundnut all-you warnt when we finish." Geraldine signalled to Wheeler. "Go bring some bowls from d'kitchen."

Standing in the kitchen, Wheeler ran her eyes along the

pale laminate counter, the blue overhead cupboards.

"Jus look by d'sink!" Geraldine called out. Wheeler crossed the room. "Y'get dem?"

Coming back out, Wheeler handed one of the Pyrex bowls to Donelle. She studied him as she sat down.

They had arrived at an economical account of what they'd heard in Bounce's family yard: Floyd di' miss out on sumting; he di' blame Tant'Celeste. An account with no mention of Innez, no Edith Michelle. An account steering clear of the dark, a darkness they sensed in big people's lives.

Floyd di' miss out on sumting. It was all they would say if they revisited what Bounce had said, revisited it between themselves.

Hands inside her bowl, Wheeler started shelling. Geraldine had dropped a fistful of the roasted groundnuts into each of their bowls. From a few steps down, Wheeler glanced back at her aunt. There was a glimmer of sweat under Geraldine's bottom lip, like a leftover smile.

"Tant'Geldine?"

Geraldine's head lifted.

"All-you used to sit an talk behind d'house when all-you was little?"

A hint of curiosity appeared on Geraldine's solid, square face. "Back dere was jus mud an stone den. We dint sit back dere much. We *used* t'sit out on d'rocks under d'trees."

And Wheeler saw her aunts: Celeste, Innez and Geraldine, all of them seated on the jumpy kitchen yard. "Meh mudda used t'sit wid all-you?" she asked, the question tentative in her throat.

"Y-es, she used t'sit out dere too."

Hands silent in her lap, Geraldine spied on Wheeler from the corner of her eye. She appeared to be listening for what else her niece might say. Nothing came.

"Yer sisters okay?"

She *sisters?*

"Dey does gang up on me... an *lie!*"

Geraldine's brown eyes lingered on Wheeler's face. "Don't fall out wid yer sisters."

Wheeler blinked then looked away. She lowered her head under the weight of that deep brown stare.

"Tant'Geldine, all-you going f'a next drive?" Donelle asked. He twisted towards the view of the lane. The car was gone. Morgan was at work.

Geraldine shook her head. "We in going yet. Ah go tell Celeste when." Mopping the sweat from her hairline with the back of her hand, she said, "Easter soon come. Ah making groundnut cake. Ah go save some f'all-you—"

"We get we kite make awready!"

"True? Who making kite f'all-you?"

"Jon-a-ton," Donelle mumbled, not saying any more, as if to say more would reveal what Bounce had said. Donelle's hooded eyes found Wheeler. She looked away, seeing her own disquiet reflected on his face.

They'd kept the visit to Bounce's yard to themselves. Wheeler understood what Bounce had said was a secret. It was a secret because no one else had ever told them.

Bounce in care *wha* he say!

She kept her wary head bent.

Leaving for home, rising up to the crest of the lane, the noise of the street gate clattered in Wheeler's ears. The sunken view reappeared: Clarkton Road, Wharf Road, the gazing church tower, points on a landscape that had become more and more familiar as the months had gone by. The sights she'd been used to, the life with her mother, overtaken by these things.

Donelle slowed down – more or less at the same spot where they'd watched the Easter kite with Jonathan. "He go bring we kite Sunday. We only hav d'tail t'find." Looking back towards the walls of their aunt's bluish-green house, he appeared uncomfortable. "Jonaton go paper dem… He goan finish dem," he said, as if once more regretful at having mentioned the kites in the first place.

Wheeler's eyes followed Donelle's. She was only part-hearing what he said.

40

Good Friday morning. After church, Donelle hovered beside her at the kitchen sink, waiting his turn for a drink of water. Tiptoeing, reaching – part-reaching – Wheeler held an enamel cup under the tap, water spilling. She bumped against Donelle as they changed over.

Floyd burst out from a cubicle under the stairs. "All-you making kite? Who tell all-you Bounce is fren t'*any*body inside dis house... h-uh? Bounce in fren t'nobody in dis house."

Donelle dropped his cup in the sink. He had his eyes on his older brother.

Wheeler tried handing Donelle her cup. He didn't take it.

"Tink dat *ma-co* hav d'*guts* t'come up here an chat shit in meh face?" Floyd grew close, broad face sweating, veins jumping in his neck. "Y'all tink all-you can do whatever all-you warnt?" Floyd frowned, blocking their way. He then turned his attention to Celeste.

Near-invisible at the side counter, Celeste stiffened. She looked round. She and Floyd appeared to be communicating with one another, eyes serving as tongues.

"Bounce in nobody t'nobody in dis house! Y'tink dat *maco* hav d'*guts* t'come an chat *shit* up *here*?" Spittle gathered at the corner of Floyd's mouth. He unbuckled his belt and yanked it off his waist.

Donelle bolted, throwing over a stool as he went.

Floyd reached in and grabbed Wheeler, swishing the belt. The cup of water fell from her hand. Floyd whacked her on the front of her legs. Wheeler fell forward onto the floor. She tried scurrying away on her hands.

Donelle di' get way… she goan get-t—

"Come! Ah jus starting. Stay right dere – y'tink is play ah playing?"

Celeste looked away.

The angry belt whipped and yelped at the side of Wheeler's head. Buttocks. Back. Bony elbow.

Again.

Back. Buttocks. Leg.

She rose up off her stomach, resorted to her hands and knees, dragging her wounded leg.

Floyd followed her, arm raised, lashing down.

"Tant'Celeste! Tant'Celeste…"

Still the belt found her.

Somebody started up wailing from far away – she didn't know who, didn't know where—

"Tink yer ant can help you?" laughed the belt, teeth yakking and biting.

Wheeler swung round on the floor, crashing into the stool.

The sickening wailing continued. Floyd lifted the belt, whipped it down across Wheeler's back and bare thighs.

Covering her mouth, Celeste darted from the counter and ran out of the room.

Sweat raced down Floyd's face, beaded round his throat. He lowered the belt, watching Celeste go.

41

Someone was still wailing. The high-pitched bawling spiralled up the kitchen stairwell. Wheeler screwed and squeezed her already tightened eyes.

Adele and Hesta attempted to soothe her. "Come. Le' we go." They helped her off the rough kitchen floor then steered her towards the bottom steps with motherly care.

"D'toilet. *D'toi-let*!" Wheeler said.

The wailing stopped.

Her sisters remained either side of her, allowing Wheeler to find her way down. They caught one another's eye.

"Why d'hell he hit her—"

"Wha he hit her for?"

"Da *crimi*-nal!" one of them said.

In the bedroom they urged Wheeler to sit down, nudging her to the side of the bed.

Wheeler recoiled. Remained as she was.

"Jus le' we take off y'dress."

Wheeler shrugged them off. The striped dress was moist with her fluids – blood, dribble, urine, tears.

"Le' we jus help you." Adele gave her an encouraging stroke. Arm by arm, she and Hesta lifted up the dress.

"Meh ribbon!"

They released the dark green hair ribbon from where it had become caught on a button.

Wheeler started lowering herself and then stopped. Pressing her weight into her palms, she eased her behind onto the bed.

"Le' we help."

They removed her shoes and socks and dropped them next to the dress. Wheeler sat drooped forward in her panties.

"How he could beat we sister like dat?"

"Why dey hav we sister in dey commesse?"

Wheeler sobbed as her sisters manoeuvred the rest of her onto the bed, her foggy eyes following the movement of Adele's mouth.

Adele carried on talking. "Dis whole *place* in a mess, is wha y'need t'know. A mess. Dey hav one set o' tebbay going on since Floyd go in we ant bedroom."

Wheeler's attention started draining away. Howls and blows played on in her mind. A toppling kitchen stool.

"We mudda in warnt t'leave us here, but—"

Hesta gave Adele a cautionary look.

Wheeler cut herself off from Adele and Hesta. She had given them as much of her attention as she could. She started focusing on what her body was doing.

Pain broke away from pain, distinct and clear, set loose by a simple turn of her neck. A pain-syrup spilled down the side of her face. A lighted fuse, a bright tinsel of agony rampaged down the centre of her back. Pain everywhere.

"Y'mus write we mudda, y'mus tell her wha happen," Wheeler cried out.

This put a stop to her sisters' muttering.

"Ah go tell her. Try an rest," Adele answered. She and Hesta started leaving the room.

"Ah taut y'say he carnt hit me?" Wheeler's voice was splintered and worn.

Neither Adele nor Hesta looked back.

Wheeler picked up the discussion with her body. She sensed a tender, determined uprising under the surface of her skin, the creeping, early onslaught of swellings and welts. Searching for some part of her that might have escaped the belt, she eased half-naked over to her right.

She lay still, unmoving. She could sense everything. Downstairs there was a row percolating, an angry voice then a quieter one.

Time twisted around itself, retracted and elongated.

Innez appeared. Then Innez was gone. Quiet all over the house.

Waking up from a deep sleep, Wheeler opened her eyes. Innez appeared again. Her fraught, bulbous head seemed to bounce against the slope of a hill. Wheeler wondered where she was.

Innez's eyes studied Wheeler's face, roved up and down, undertaking a survey of some kind. Someone brought Wheeler a plate from a place by the back window. Lunch.

Recognising Hesta, Wheeler still wondered where she was.

"Y'in hav t'eat it now."

Sweat festered on Wheeler's scrawny chest. She frowned. "But ah *warnt* t'eat it now."

Hesta stood holding the plate.

Wheeler prepared herself. Placed her weight on her elbow and tilted up. Pain eddied around her buttocks as she edged round to the side of the bed.

Hesta handed Wheeler the plate. Wheeler's nostrils twitched. Stewfish. She could smell it now. Her saliva loosened. She lifted a spoon of fish and rice to her mouth. As she lowered the spoon, her mind swam with images of what had happened. She watched as Donelle escaped—

She in try an run too?

Wheeler rummaged in vain for an answer, hands shaking, gripping on to the plate.

Floyd di' yank out he belt.

Wheeler watched that too. She recalled being astonished by the first blow, recalled the falling, the kneeling.

She di' call Tant'Celeste.

The memory was vivid and startling.

She di' call Tantie Celeste name again.

Wheeler started chewing.

She ant did run.

After easing into a housedress, Wheeler crept down the stairs.

Jonathan was out on the veranda. She told herself she'd go out and sit with him when she came back upstairs. Returned from the toilet, she went back into the room and folded herself onto the bed.

He appeared to the side of the bed. He had Donelle with him. Time was up to its old tricks again. Wheeler's brows twitched.

She in know if d'two o' dem di' standing dere. Or… if she di' remembering dem from somewhere else—

She examined the pair with mistrust.

"Bounce say y'can hav a big kite now," Jonathan said.

Wheeler studied him, his likeable face right there in the space where Innez's bigger head had been.

But he mudda dint say a ting.

"Y'can hav a big kite now."

She heard the words but took no comfort from what he was saying. She had not seen Donelle since the beating. His expression was sympathetic as well as gloomy. He said, "He goan string it. Y'can hav a big kite now."

Wheeler squinted at him: He di' say d'same ting Jonaton did say.

At some point the brothers left. Two wary lines of suspicion, Wheeler's eyes disappeared under their lids.

Floyd's voice repeated in her ear: *Y'all tink all-you can do whatever all-you warnt...?* Having assumed the beating was meant for Donelle, Wheeler now thought it might have been for either of them.

42

"H-*m…mm*." A squeak from Wheeler after a night's sleep. "*Ohw-w*!" Lying heavy on her back, she tested out her arms, legs, *neck*! Her body had become its own ripe, tormented world. "Ah-h…ah warnt t'pee."

Adele nudged Hesta. "*Wha?* Ah in lying on her!"

Hesta rolled out of the way. Wheeler remained on the bed.

Adele said, "Y'jus hav t'get up." She climbed over Wheeler.

The urge to get up, the urge to stay in bed alternated in Wheeler's mind, with something wishful in between.

Nutting di' happen, she dint get licks yesterday.

"Y'jus hav t'come on." Adele reached in and rolled Wheeler out of the bed.

"Ar-rr-rr!" There was no deciding which part of her hurt the most.

Adele supported Wheeler to the stairs, arms around her. They eased their way down. At the lower steps, Wheeler stared out to the yard. No Celeste.

After the toilet, Adele gestured Wheeler towards the shower.

"Law-w-d!" The sting of cold water ignited a whole new kind of distress: a battle between icy needles and her bruise-ripened self. She almost fell.

Wide-eyed and chattering, Wheeler looked for Adele. She was gone.

Wheeler hugged herself and inched back under the water. After the initial shock, her bare body started taking pleasure in the confusion, the cold water and her pain now giving way to one another. The healing water started numbing the criss-cross of welts on her skin.

Adele's head appeared above the swing doors. She held out a towel. "Jus mop, don't rub yerself."

After the shower, Wheeler paused in the kitchen doorway. Let out of the coop, the hens were now feeding in the yard. She watched them peck and shove one another as they ate. Celeste was reaching into the coop, collecting the eggs.

She in see she ant til now. Tant'Celeste in come an look f'her. Tant'*Innez* di' come.

Cold water ran like tears as Adele took her turn in the shower.

After managing to dress herself, Wheeler perched on the side of the bed. Hesta sat at the other end, plaiting her own hair. Adele came in and Hesta looked at her. Adele searched Hesta's face. Hesta got up and turned her back.

Black spots whirled before Wheeler's eyes as she swivelled her head from one to the other.

261

Dey did quarrel bout sumting? Wha dey quarrel for?

"F-f-for *Christ* sake!" Adele stumped her foot against the floor, thrusting her leg into a pair of panties.

Whatever mood Hesta in, Adele di' in it too.

Backing away from the cupboard, Adele hopped, clutching her foot, one leg in her panties, one leg out.

"M'neck hutting me," Wheeler grumbled. The effect of the cold water fading, her aches had started up again.

Adele said, "Y'neck bound to pain you. Every way's goan pain you. If not more dan yesterday—"

"Y'tell we mudda?"

Hesta fixed her eyes on Adele. Adele hesitated. "Is only Sat'day. Ah in get a chance yet."

Hair part-plaited, Hesta reached for her bath towel.

"Why it mus hut more dan yesterday?"

"Jonaton in d'shower," Adele warned.

Hesta stormed out of the room.

An hour later there was an unexpected rattle at the window. Wheeler's eyes turned in her head. Nobody. Just a gentle breeze. Plus the light of a yellow day.

The lure of a Saturday wander began tugging at her. Mid-morning, she rolled herself upright on the bed. Her swollen shins rebelled as she pressed her feet into the slithering flip-flops. She went to find Donelle.

She saw him coming along the bottom entrance. Wheeler's calves pulsed as she spun back round. She held on to the side of the house with both hands and shuffled down the veranda steps. "Don-elle!" She hadn't realised she was hoarse. "Don-elle!" she called to him again. It looked as if he might carry on drifting up the Cut.

He turned towards the house. The little furrow in his brow twisted in discomfort as Wheeler limped out.

"How come he say ah can hav a big kite?"

Donelle lowered his eyes. Some things didn't need an answer, his saddened features seemed to say.

They sat together on the steps, waiting for Wheeler to get herself together so they could take off. They gazed into the deep shaft of the Cut blinking, as the concrete light flickered, as distant figures criss-crossed below.

She sister di' awready gone t'buy messages.

Wheeler's attention drifted off to Wharf Road.

Donelle's expression brightened a little. "We kite coming tomorrow." His smile broadened. "Hgh, Jonaton hav a church dress belonging t'we mudda. He say he goan *tear it up, oui*, an make tail!"

Wheeler doubled up.

"Yer leg still hutting you?"

She nodded, still folded forward.

Grabbing hold of the terrace wall, Wheeler hobbled back towards the house. Donelle climbed into the sunlight without her. The long veranda hovered in darkness and light. When she looked up, Floyd was standing there.

"*Ah-h!*" Pain, humiliation – *fear* – blitzed through

Wheeler. She froze, her body too sickened to run.

Floyd was dressed for work: khaki longpants, short-sleeved khaki shirt. He hesitated at first, then turned round and went back into the house.

In bed she listened to the sounds inside and outside the house: rustling in the bushes, tiny chirps and silences. Wheeler worried over who might still be home and who out.

Dropping into a heavy sleep, black water surrounded her. From the quayside, points around the dockyard began to appear: low warehouses, outlying buildings, narrow turns. The sounds of machines. She was in the midst of a slow-moving march.

We mudda going.

Her mind could manage only one thought in the dream. And she told it to the people next to her. "We mudda going."

The procession veered toward a dough-coloured building. Wheeler glided along with the others. A smiling Miss Eadie was already in there, a cardboard grip of bananas opened at her feet. Miss Eadie turned round and smiled. "Y'mudda getting ready f'church, she go come when d'service finish."

A bright conveyor belt shot into the night on the quayside. Wheeler was alongside her sisters. They were waiting for their mother.

Adele rushed at the gangway, bawling. Steeples, towers,

bridges reared up, blocking her way. She couldn't go round them. By the time the other passengers and her mother appeared overhead, they were already waving down from England.

Waking up, Wheeler gaped at the light coming in crooked along the ceiling, with shadows of leaves waving and struggling in it.

Somewhere a fly was fretting. Her eyes tried to find it.

She had slept late into the afternoon. Activity in the house had continued during her absence. There was now movement and sounds in various parts of the house. Her stomach ached at the smell of baking coming from downstairs.

She tried sitting up. A look of doubt appeared on Wheeler's face. She began sinking. An awareness of something had arrived from nowhere: The church hat and dress remembered from a distance; the way her mother laughed...

D'sound o' she mudda voice.

Wheeler stared at the window, at the housefly fussing. She realised she could no longer remember her mother's face.

They'd left Wheeler's lunch covered on the floor by the bed.

In the evening she went downstairs unaided, with her weight on the leg that hadn't been whipped. The old stairs protested in unfamiliar ways due to the unusual way they were being taken.

A part of her mind was still in the dream world: the sky-high banana boat materialised then faded; she heard the screech of the jolting conveyor belt; a jokey Miss Eadie kept on calling her. And still Wheeler could not conjure her mother's face.

As she lowered herself on the upper stairs, Donelle's eyes pointed her towards the bottom steps. Floyd was in his place. Wheeler stopped herself from looking at him.

The usual Saturday night: the air rich with coconut buns and the smell of bread cooling on the counter; the scent of cocoa tea and kerosene, all of it mixed up with the evening meal.

When the call came to get their plates, it came from Adele.

Her first time coming to eat on the stairs since what had happened, and Celeste was not there. Wheeler struggled round, remembering something, and looked up. She thought she'd heard Celeste's voice in Innez's bedroom.

Jonathan had been sent up with Wheeler's meal. A plate of okra and saltfish and a nipple roll sat at the corner of her eye.

Once more in the world of her soupy mind, Wheeler glanced from the plate to Jonathan as he went down the stairs. She had not seen him come up. She slipped the plate onto her lap, not moving her head.

She stared at Jonathan as on something in her dream. When Donelle took his mother's meal upstairs, Wheeler experienced the motion of him climbing by as a slow whisper in her ear.

Sitting still had spared her the pain in her neck. But she couldn't make the muddle in her mind go away.

43

Easter Sunday. Lemony swathes of sunlight circled the hills, swirling from right to left and straight on out to sea. The sky empty, nothing swaying or flapping in any direction. The noise of seagulls scavenging above the water had grown fainter as the birds retreated towards the docks. Wheeler gazed out from the veranda.

She dint tell she sisters she di' forget she mudda. She di' stop tinking bout d'dream.

Some aspects of her mother still remained. She still recalled her standing out on the porch after coming home from the market. Her mother saying what she'd cooked for them before leaving for work. Talking to them in the sitting room on the night that she left. Now, however, those memories came without her mother's face.

Earlier, as Wheeler sat easing on her church shoes, Innez had wandered into the room. Gazing at the ironed dress laid out on the bed, she said, "Y'in hav t'go t'Sunday school. Y'should stay here."

Wheeler's eyes had moistened, her jaw tightened as she'd watched Innez stroll out of the room.

Tant'Innez dint say she sorry, she in talk bout wha Floyd di' do.

Wheeler's right side complained from standing. She pressed her weight against the veranda wall. She pictured herself walking alongside Jonathan and Donelle, none of them talking. The sense of them walking alongside one another soothed her. As much as she disliked Sunday school, she wished she'd been allowed to go with them.

She searched for Jonathan and Donelle in the gaps along Russell Street, between layers of red galvanised rooftops where the road turned. She wondered where they were.

Wheeler set her sights on the opening at the bottom of the Mill Street shortcut, a place Donelle and Jonathan would have to come to on their way. She placed her chin on her folded arms and squinted, making her area of focus as tight as possible and waited for them. A woman and a child crossed Wheeler's tightened plane of vision—

Not *dem*!

Unsuspecting prey waltzing into a trap, figures she didn't recognise.

Though it hadn't been long since the brothers had left the house, she grew impatient. She was tired of wondering where they were, wondering what was keeping them. Wheeler pretended she was walking ahead of them. She imagined herself running up the drain alley, tearing along Mill Street, with the Methodist church up in the distance. She saw herself rushing up Churchway, other children racing beside her, all of them arriving in the schoolroom together.

She woulnt miss Sunday school. But she di' like running in d'schoolyard afterwards.

Wheeler straightened up and switched her attention from the elementary schoolyard to the little fishing boats, blobs of colour on the edge of the shore.

Jonaton di' say he goan bring she kite back when he come—

Something dropped behind her, inside the house. Wheeler's body stiffened. Floyd was in his bedroom. Her breathing slowed down.

He di' start moving bout.

She pressed herself against the house and waited. Through the side sitting room window she watched Floyd stride out of his bedroom. She waited a moment more, then eased into the open. Watching Floyd sweep into the kitchen stairwell, she recalled the twist and speed of his belt. Bitter thoughts went through Wheeler's mind. She grabbed onto the window ledge.

Y'mudda leave y'wid Innez, she sister di' say. *Y'mudda in leave y'wid Floyd!*

As if in flight they came.

Returned from Sunday school, Jonathan and Donelle dashed into the room with a flourish resembling the kites they were brandishing. She hadn't seen them walk into the shortcut, or up to the elementary school. She had stopped looking.

"Tek it!" Jonathan said.

"Is yours, tek it."

The brothers' shared excitement brought Wheeler to her feet. She no longer cared *which* side of her hurt. She reached out for the kite Jonathan was offering. He'd been true to his word. A shrill constellation of yellow and red and pink paper, the eight-sided kite was almost as tall as her.

"D'kite big f'so! Bigger 'n mine." Donelle said.

"It *big*."

"All o' we hav we kite now," said Jonathan, holding up his own oversized kite as proof. A smaller version of the green and blue and pink kite hung at Donelle's side. The clear, translucent colours transferred a watery delicacy to objects in the room. The bedroom walls and floor shimmered with shapes and colours.

Donelle and Jonathan stepped back as Wheeler held up her kite. The pink-yellow-red kite floated lantern-like in the little room, its paper rustling.

The brothers had approached via the sitting room – past Floyd's bedroom – as if Jonathan no longer cared *who* knew about the enterprise he and Bounce were running. Taking the kite away from Wheeler, Jonathan held it aloft on its string moorings. "Ah string it meh self," he said with satisfaction. "Is best if y'string it wid twine."

Arriving back from church, Hesta pushed past Jonathan, sweating, saying a series of things: "Whey all-you get dem kite? Whey all-you bin? All-you go, na. Sch-uu!"

Jonathan handed Wheeler back her kite. Bundled to a ball to prevent it from dragging, the kite's tail dangled underneath it looking obscene.

"Why y'giving we sister dat big kite?" Adele asked, coming in. "All-you take dem kite outa here. Le' we get change."

"Ah go take it up t'd'Guide Hall f'you," said Jonathan.

Wheeler's features sank. She fell back onto the bed as the brothers left, taking her kite with them.

44

She never made it to the Guide Hall and would never fly the giant kite.

Starting with a light showering in late morning out by the fort, the waterfront had become deluged with kites by early afternoon. Multicoloured kites had started appearing in the distance like incoming rain, twitching and wobbling, until a light veil hung right across the bay.

Wheeler waited to leave. Donelle and Jonathan had already gone. As her sisters came out, Innez shouted for Adele. "*Yes, Tant'Innez!* Go, ah soon come," she said.

Moments later, hurrying down the veranda steps, Adele called to Hesta and Wheeler. "Come back," she said, eyes on Wheeler. "Best y'stay here."

"But ah feeling better. Ah warnt t'come!"

Adele responded to Wheeler in the voice of someone else: "If y'in feeling good enough t'go t'church, then y'carnt go out d' house an fly a kite." Adding, "Y'carnt come."

"But ah did *warnt* t'go t'Sunday school." Wheeler was wearing her church dress, green ribbons in her hair.

Hesta started walking away, shaking her head.

"But… Ah warnt t'fly meh kite!"

"Innez say y'carnt come. Y'hav to stay here."

Hesta and Adele took off up the Cut. There were people climbing ahead of them, everyone in their good clothes.

More adults and children appeared, carrying kites uphill.

Trapped on the veranda, Wheeler stared at them. All sense of occasion drained out of her. She felt cut off from the other children talking and running uphill. Wheeler backed away to the sitting room doorway, not sure she should let anyone see her.

She imagined the scenes in the Guide Hall grounds: Donelle tearing up and down the bank, avoiding other kids, all of them trying to launch their kite just like him. Grown people shouting: *All-you giv it line, na! Giv it line!* Donelle's green and blue kite bucking and flying, ducking, slamming on the ground.

Older teenagers stood liming at the top of the lane, outside the Guide Hall walls, setting their kites off from there. Her sisters shouting and joking with them, their voices soaring. And Jonathan—

Wheeler's lips tensed.

He di' giv she kite t'Donelle. He di' go out on d'lane after he di' help he brudda start it.

A tight screw of her face.

She dint hav t'be up dere to *know* Donelle di' flying she kite. He di' hand over he kite to somebody else – flying she kite instead o' he own – when he hear she in coming.

274

Anger ate away at Wheeler's insides. She struggled to be kind-hearted, to remember how Donelle hadn't minded when Jonathan had handed her the giant kite. She tried but failed. She shuffled off to the bedroom, eased onto the bed and curled in on herself.

Meanwhile, up in the Guide Hall grounds, Donelle continued to give the kite line. He too was struggling.

She di' *sure* he di' getting drag about. Trying t'stop he line getting tangle up wid udda people kite!

The long uneven floorboards outside the bedroom started complaining. Wheeler lifted her head. She tracked the weighty movements on the landing and beyond, the sound of Innez leaving via the sitting room.

Dey di' take she kite away... now Tant'Innez di' going in d'Guide Hall grounds jus like e'rybody else!

Hot tears bubbled down Wheeler's face. She stared at the vacant space where the giant kite had been.

45

When evening came, Adele and Hesta returned to the house. She heard them calling back to other people as they came in off the Cut. Wheeler sat up on the bed. Primed.

"All-you di' hav a good time? All-you come back."

An uneasy look passed between Adele and Hesta as they strolled into the room. Hesta crossed over to her usual place by the window. Adele eased down on the bed. "So-so." She seemed unable to meet Wheeler's eyes.

"Donelle an dem in come back yet, jus all-you. Y'in see dem?"

Hesta fidgeted. Cautious at first, she started giving an account of the time they'd had: "Donelle di' fly y'kite to kingdom come!"

Adele looked at Hesta. "Jonaton di' help him."

"Ah in warnt to live here no more."

"He di' hav t'get it flying—"

"Dey di' hav all kinda kite—"

Her sisters continued their exchange, repeating details each had already given. Wheeler's voice had been soft. Still, both appeared to have heard.

"Wha she saying?"

"Ah in warnt t'stay here no more."

Hesta lashed out at Wheeler: "Y'tink it easy f'us? Baking, cooking – doing all dey work!"

"Ah in lissening t'you. Ah in warnta stay here."

Adele shut the bedroom door. "All-you keep all-you voice down."

Hesta kept going, raking into Wheeler: "It in easy f'us *eida*! Is not jus you—"

"*Hush* up," Adele warned her.

Hesta looked out of the window. She appeared to have calmed down. "We hav t'do wha we mudda warnt," she muttered.

Wheeler slid off the bed, as if wanting to get away there and then. "Ah not staying here no more."

"We mudda gone in Ingland f'*us*." Hesta.

Wheeler shoved herself in against the end cupboard. Her voice became a ragged plea. "Ahh-ah in staying here no mo! Ah warnt t' stay wid Tantie Geldine an Uncl'Morgan."

Hesta grunted. "We mudda in warnt us living wid dem—"

"Y'*lie*. All-you does *lie*! Y'say Floyd carnt hit me. Y'say" – Wheeler pointed – "y'say Hesta in *teef* d'money!"

Hesta looked away.

Adele's body sagged. "Ah-h… never *believe* he would hit you." She shook her head a little. The weight of Adele's admission hung over the room. "Come out from dere."

She held out her hand to Wheeler.

Wheeler grabbed hold of the headrail.

"Come an siddown. Le' we talk t'you."

"Ah in trust all-you. Ah going an live wid Uncl'Morgan and Tantie Geldine."

"Is d'truth." Adele glanced at Hesta. "Y'carnt go an live dere. We mudda in warnt us t'go an live wid dem. She in warnt us t'go an live wid dem… because of you."

Wheeler trained her eyes on Adele, steadied herself. Sizing up her sisters, she turned from Adele to Hesta and then back again. There was an awful finality in the way they looked: *Because of you.* Her heartbeat quickened.

"Is true," Adele continued. "Because of you. When we mudda leave f'Ingland, she dint warnt us t'stay wid dem – no matter d'commesse dey hav going on here." Adele raised her eyes and looked around, seeming to take in the entire house, not just the room. "When time come f'd'tree of us t'go t'Ingland, we mudda di' tink Geldine and Morgan would try an keep you… dey woulnt make y'go if y'dint warnt to."

Pain returned to Wheeler's neck, intensified in her legs. She longed for the comfort of the bed. "Ah in lissening!"

Why she mus lissen? Hesta in like her.

Wheeler glared at Hesta.

D'two o'dem does lie! Dey does take up f'one anudda an *lie*!

"When we farda leave, Tantie Geldine an Uncl'Morgan di' ask t'raise you."

Dey did ask t'*raise* her?

"T'help we mudda," added Adele. "E'rybody know dey di' ask t'raise you. Y'was still small. We mudda di' tell dem no."

"*Ah* in know." Tantie Geldine, Uncl'Morgan talking – *asking* in d'house in town?

Wheeler couldn't imagine that.

"We mudda di' warnt us t'stay *here*," Adele said. "She di' decide t'*pay* Tant'Innez t'keep us. T'keep all of us."

Wheeler struggled to think why that part wouldn't be true. Moving away from the cupboard, she dropped onto the bed.

"Here – dry yer eyes."

"Ah in *warnt* t'dry m'eyes." She pulled away to the far side of the bed.

The room had gone quiet. Wheeler could hear voices away from the house. Someone ran down the kitchen stairs. She could hear footsteps in Donelle and Jonathan's bedroom.

Adele and Hesta had started getting ready to go down. There was an air of solemnity in the way they changed out of their out-of-house clothes: Adele hanging up her pleated skirt, rearranging the folds; Hesta stepping out of her dress and carrying it to the bed, lining up the button holes, buttoning the dress and folding it away.

Adele raised an eyebrow after checking on Wheeler lying curled on the bed. Hesta returned Adele's look and then shrugged. Adele mumbled, "Ah in warnt t'leave everyting til tomorrow. Ah goan whiten we Keds."

Hesta slipped out of the room after Adele. Wheeler's eyes followed them.

Dey does lie.

She remained in the careful quiet her sisters had created. Wheeler repeated the words with waning conviction.

"Dey does lie."

46

There was the sound of a radio in the distance. Gone was the whistling silence of Lent.

The next morning Wheeler and Donelle stared out from the veranda. They both looked as if they were avoiding something, something neither wanted the other to hear. An unhappy secret lingered in Wheeler's mind. Her eyes dropped to the lumberyard.

"Ah sorry y'kite mash-up," said Donelle, regret in his eyes. He was focusing neither on the water nor the view. "D'kite headstrong. It get tangle up in udda people line."

They'd each had a less than successful kite season.

"Dey did call tell Jonaton t'come back. D'kite mash up fore he come."

As predicted, Donelle had handed over his smaller kite to someone else. Wheeler reflected on what he was saying.

"Ah dint hav nutting t'fly." He turned to face her. "D'kid run way wid me own kite."

"Y'in see whey he go?"

Donelle lowered his voice. "Ah din trouble him. Jonaton say ah carnt take back d'kite."

Wheeler looked away, her own conscience troubling her. Unable to look at Donelle, she stared at her tiny wrists flopping over the veranda ledge.

The night before, she had drifted ghostlike down to supper, everything feeling disconnected: banisters cut off from posts, stair posts from stairs.

"We ready!"

When the call came to collect her plate, she had floated into the well of the kitchen, disbelieving her own presence once she was there.

Celeste stood with her back to Wheeler, shuffling at the stove. Wheeler's confusion deepened.

How she di' hear Tant'Celeste voice up in Tant'Innez bedroom? Wha dey saying?

Jumbie-like, Wheeler had wafted back up the stairs, had sat staring at her plate.

Now, she knitted her fingers together where they dangled over the ledge, and decided:

She not telling Donelle wha she sisters di' say.

To tell him would mean revealing her own secret – that she didn't want to live there any more.

"Wha?"

"Tant'Geldine. She di' up in d'Guide ground," Donelle repeated. "She say she di' keep d'groundnut cake f'us, we mus come get dem."

Wheeler pictured her uncle and aunt in the Guide Hall grounds. Everybody up there. Floyd as well.

"Le' we go get we groundnut cake."

Wheeler hesitated.

Dey d'try an take her from she mudda! She in warnt t'go dere.

Taking her time, she trailed after Donelle towards the veranda steps. There was discomfort in her mind and in her body. She had remained bed-bound, more or less, since Good Friday. There was a reminder in her neck as she lifted her head and looked up. Her lower back grouched and complained as she started climbing the Cut.

"Come back!"

Wheeler stopped. She turned her whole body around.

Adele leaned out from the veranda. "Come!"

Hesta came running from behind the house, added: "So we can wash yer hair."

H-uh. She sisters trying t'sound *nice*!

Wheeler levelled her eyes at both of them. She remained on the Cut. She waited a long, disenchanted moment, facing uphill. She looked as if she might carry on in spite of them.

"Go on," she told Donelle. "Ah not coming."

Mid-morning. Large fluffy clouds drifted overhead, nudged along by the breeze. The sky above vast and white, the bay a satisfying blue. Adele placed a towel around Wheeler's shoulders, having finished washing her hair. Steering her away from the house, she led Wheeler towards the volcanic yard. Soon after, they invited her into the circle at the back of the house.

Hesta was already waiting on the protrusion of rocks where, together, she and Adele would write their latest letter to their mother. Now, Adele pointed Wheeler to Hesta's usual place. Wheeler made a face.

She in warnt t'sit wid dem.

Hesta stood up. Adele hustled Wheeler towards the spot. Wheeler sat on the rocks. Feet in the gutter, Hesta settled herself across from them.

"Whey you an Donelle going?"

Wheeler's eyes followed Hesta's to the hillside steps.

Whey? "We jus going."

"Donelle can go f'heself." Hesta's voice softened as she turned to Wheeler. "Look, nobody in saying y'carnt go by we uncle an we ant—"

"All-you say ah carnt live dere!" Wheeler rounded on her sister, though leery herself about going to the house.

Adele twitched. "We mudda hav good reason f'wha she do. F'not leaving us dere—"

"She in decide t'leave us in dis house f'no reason."

Adele started combing out Wheeler's hair. Wheeler's eyes lingered on Hesta, long legs curled up in front of her, hair pulled up on her bully's head.

"O-ww!"

"Sorry."

Don't fall out wid yer sisters. Geraldine's words came into her head. Catching on, Wheeler gaped.

She mudda an Tantie Geldine di' fall out! Tant'Geldine

di' fall out wid she own sister. Dey mudda!

Geraldine's words echoed against the cracked concrete ground, all of them now worthy of inspection:

Don't fall out…

Y'mudda di' bring you once…

Y'was still little…

Eyes wide open, Wheeler lifted her head. Geraldine's words darted into the clouds.

"Lower yer head." The words clattered back down as Wheeler lowered her head.

How y'sisters...

Y'mudda di' bring y'here once...

Wheeler tried imagining her mother in Geraldine's yellow kitchen leaning against the counter, eyes roaming around.

Her sisters were talking.

"Look, it different. Me an Hesta big."

"Is easy f'little chil'ren t'forget dey mudda."

Listening to this, Wheeler bit her treacherous lip.

"Y'tink tings easy?" said Hesta, voice patronising and slow.

She in say tings easy!

Wheeler swivelled to face Adele. "When we mudda sending f'us?"

"We in know."

"How you in know?"

"We in know—"

"How y'in know?"

"*In a few years' time*!" barked Hesta, congenial no more.

Wheeler turned back round. Adele continued combing, completing one, two, another plait.

In a few years' time!

The low-hanging clouds started breaking apart. A purple ache radiated out from Wheeler's buttocks, which felt flat and sore.

Hesta gave Wheeler a telling look. "Some people dey go in Ingland, dey in *never* sen f'dey big chil'ren. All o' we hav t'go together."

Wheeler heard the crash of the kitchen stool thrown over by Donelle. She felt the wrenching of her arm once more.

"Together," added Hesta.

Wheeler thought about Floyd.

Wha if he keep beating her?

It had started raining at night, light-sounding swishing rain reawakening the earth. Wheeler stared at the terraced garden, at the emaciated bloodroot shrub that had started turning green.

"Wha if Floyd keep beating me?" she asked.

Leaving the comb in Wheeler's hair, Adele kept on plaiting. Hesta glared.

Wha if he keep beating her?

Hesta and Wheeler's eyes met.

"Y'mus try not t'do nutting wrong," Hesta said.

47

Standing by the concrete sink, Wheeler looked out.

She dint know how she goan stay outa trouble. How she goan know before she do sumting wrong?

She stared towards a cargo ship in the harbour, continued to stare at the stern.

She mudda di' tell dem all o' she biznis fore she go. Not her. She hav t' do wha she mudda warnt.

The banana boat had returned the week before. Cruising towards the harbour, the vast white ship had appeared reduced – dull and grey under a changing sky.

That night Wheeler had caught first Adele then Hesta pausing as they walked past the kitchen sink. She had slowed down on the stairs, catching them staring towards the yellow cabin lights outside the window.

She sisters di' holding dey supper staring at d'banana boat. Maybe dey miss we mudda too.

As if sensing Wheeler's eyes on her, Hesta had turned and walked away. Adele had followed her out.

Now a bird took off from the stern of the cargo ship towards the fort.

Adele thundered down the kitchen stairs. Wheeler twisted towards the house. Adele headed back up, clutching her schoolbooks to her chest. Wheeler wondered what she'd forgotten now.

Celeste slipped out of the bushes and made her way across to the house. Wheeler judged her.

She ant dint come an help when Floyd di' beat her. She di' run. She sisters di' come an help her. Tant'Celeste in never come say she sorry when she di' lying in she bed…

Wheeler gasped as Celeste got closer. The horror of the beating was written right there on Celeste's face. Wheeler's mouth widened. Celeste's devastated face told Wheeler all she'd wanted to know: Tant'Celeste di' *care*. She di' *care*.

She had not spoken to her aunt, had not looked in her face since—

Before Tantie Celeste di' run way.

In the intervening days Celeste had remained in the yard or slipped back to her room. Or—

She did… She di' hear she ant talking in Tant'Innez bedroom.

Looking at Wheeler, a small trace of compassion lightened Celeste's face.

Wheeler was left unable to speak, unable to say good morning.

"Don't pass yer time no more in dis kitchen," Celeste had once told Wheeler. Still, Floyd had caught her leaving Celeste's bedroom. He would damage *anything*.

Wheeler moved towards her aunt.

Adele swept past Celeste at the kitchen doorway. "Tant'Celeste, we going! Le' we go."

Wheeler followed Adele, stumbling round.

On the way to school, light twinkled on white Keds and shiny legs, white shirts and socks. The weekday glitter of schoolchildren making their way along the road.

Excitement flared in Wheeler's eyes. She glanced down at her shadow. She wanted to tell Adele about Celeste.

Wha she could say? She sister dint see wha happen. Dat she di' come outa d'bush. Dat she di' stop. She dint see d'look on Tant'Celeste face.

Wheeler directed a questioning eye towards Adele.

With Adele leaving the yard and disappearing under the line of the house, Celeste had at last spoken to Wheeler.

"Tant'Celeste di' tell me, 'Mind yerself,'" Wheeler told Adele. "She di' say, 'Mind yerself, do.'" There was pleasure in Wheeler's voice. "We ant di' run way, but she di' care," said Wheeler. "Not like Tant'Innez."

The metal on Adele's circle comb glinted. She didn't say anything.

"Ah di' keep outa Floyd way."

Adele swallowed. Twice. She appeared discomfited.

"He di' call Donelle from he room. He dint call loud. Ah di' go down d'stairs when ah hear him."

Adele pressed on, though they were not late. Wheeler

kept up with her. The weight of the school bag had started awakening the soreness in her arm.

They overtook younger children at the houseshop and caught up to a crowd of older boys, a salty breeze tossing Wheeler's hair ribbon. As she looked up, the sky was filled with clouds and teenage boys. She started limping. "Why y'in slow down?"

Adele slowed down, eyes aimed straight ahead. Wheeler spotted something in her sister's face.

Every time she wid she sisters, dey make her feel bad! Dey di' tell her keep outa trouble, dat she carnt live by she ant and she uncle.

She doing wha dey tell her t'do!

Approaching the cars at the police traffic box, Adele placed a protective hand on Wheeler's shoulder. Wheeler pulled away.

She didn't join in with the children hurrying up to the schoolhouse. Wheeler removed the satchel from her shoulder and let the others run past under the shadow of the flowing clouds.

After the bell, her leg now aching, she walked in, going much slower than usual. The teacher stared at her from the front of the room, then looked away, making no comment about the way Wheeler moved.

Anchoring herself at her desk, a feeling of calm came over Wheeler, reassured by what was familiar about the school: the sudden silence, here and in the neighbouring classrooms.

The teacher's eyes were on her again.

Wha she do? She dint warnt t'be in trouble.

The teacher looked away, smudged then rewrote a number on the board. Wheeler turned her stiffened neck.

Their eyes met.

"All-you… All-you know wha all-you doing." The teacher walked out of the room with a saddened look.

Late afternoon, waiting for Donelle, a tremor went through Wheeler as she spied Bounce liming with a group of boys further down.

Bounce in fren t'nobody in dis house! Nobody in dis house.

Wheeler waved back as Jonathan lifted his arm. She checked on Bounce's whereabouts.

Floyd di' hate Bounce. He better stay whey he is.

Donelle was talking to her. "Y'in save none o'yer groundnut cake?"

She shook her head. "Ah in hav no more." There was a look of tenderness on her face.

He di' go an get d'groundnut cake when she sisters di' call her back. He di' bring hers too.

Wheeler shook her head once more, not knowing what else to do.

"Oh-h," Donelle said. "Ah di' share mine wid Jonaton. But she di' make a lot."

They were now climbing further up. As he reached the top, Donelle stopped and looked to his right towards the bend in the lane leading to Morgan and Geraldine's house. *She go hav more groundnut cake left*, his hesitation seemed to say.

"Y'not coming?" Wheeler said, walking away to the left.

"Le' we go round *dis* way. See wha happ'ning."

Wheeler faced the other way.

His shirt part-open, Donelle's body pointed one way, his head the next. Wheeler stared at the ground. A wary stand-off was developing between them.

Dey di' try an take her from she mudda!

Wheeler recalled Geraldine's quiet, faraway look. She saw Morgan's eyes in the rear-view mirror.

Uncl'Morgan, how dey looking...

She heard his voice.

Dey jus looking...

We jus taking a drive...

She did like driving wid dem in d'car—

But then she heard her sisters saying: *When time come t'go t'Ingland dey woulnt make y'go!*

She walked away.

48

In the middle of the night, a commotion.

Wheeler awoke to the battle of heavy rain on the galvanised roof. And underneath it something else. Someone bawling into the noise. Things crashing. Darkness.

Her sisters were already on the move, Hesta tumbling out of bed, Adele clambering over her. They stumbled against one another in the bedroom doorway.

Wheeler swung her feet down to the floor. "Wha going on?"

"Ah in know."

Jonathan and Donelle were outside their bedroom.

She sister... she sisters di' run f'd'veranda.

A fleeting presence on the landing: Floyd heading for the kitchen stairs. "All-you stay in all-you *room!*"

The sound of rumbling. "Whey dat coming from?" she wondered out loud.

"E-dith Mi-shhhelle!"

Hearing a desperate cry, Wheeler swerved towards the veranda.

Tant'Celeste di' call f'she dead chile!

Rain flew at Wheeler. In the darkness, arms outstretched, she tapped the doorway, tapped for the veranda's edge. She found the back of one of her sisters instead.

Something crashed.

Wheeler peered over the ledge. A pale suggestion of light in the spiking, silver rain outside Celeste's bedroom.

"Tant'Celeste!"

There was someone on the move in the dark: black in black.

"Tant'Celeste – whey y'going?"

The smack of Adele hurrying then falling down the veranda steps. A light came on in a doorway further down. Rain continued to hammer the veranda roof.

Floyd then Jonathan burst out of the house into the yard, a trace of Adele chasing after them.

A distant figure flashed past in the light further down. A final, brief sighting from the veranda for Wheeler, Hesta and Donelle of their aunt escaping the family house.

49

The sun lifted its head.

Astonished, Wheeler stared at the bedroom window. The room – the rest of the house – was quiet. The night's disturbances had leached away, the sounds of mayhem, of rain walloping the roof. The noise from Celeste as she ran down the hill shouting her baby's name.

There was sunlight in the back window.

Wheeler climbed over Hesta and out of bed. She drifted out onto the landing, glanced at the veranda and then headed down the stairs.

The sky was a clean, indifferent blue. The bay was dirty, muddy with run-off from the land. A slow breeze blowing in off the sea greeted Wheeler. There was no one in the kitchen, no one approaching from under the stairs. Yet certain things remained possible.

Wheeler stood. She reeled through the times she'd spent in the kitchen with Celeste.

She ant standing close, giving her d'swizzle stick. Cracking eggs, filling d'cocoa pot as well. She ant lifting she arm, looking to rap Jonaton in he head... *Bwoy, why y'always rushing y'food?* Putting d'cocoa pot back on d'stove... *Awright, we ready!*

She looked across to the kitchen doorway, hoping Celeste might be out in the yard.

Innez appeared, standing gazing at the bay. Decked in her big nightdress, wearing her eyeglasses, Innez had not appeared the night before. She had not gone out to the veranda. Trailing back into the house, Wheeler and Donelle had milled about the landing waiting for news.

"All-you go in all-you *bed*," Hesta had told them. "Go t'bed."

Innez had not come out of her room. Now in the yard, she held herself erect. She had the bearing of a woman who had come into her own.

Wheeler stared.

Seeming to remember the feed bucket, Innez glanced down. As she scattered the chicken feed on the ground, Wheeler slipped away, drawn to Celeste's bedroom.

Wheeler surveyed the mess from the bedroom doorway in the scant ground-floor light. She studied the shape of the ransacking – both riveting and disturbing – eyes joining in the frantic, panicked hunt. She absorbed the aftermath: the striped, clawed-apart mattress upended on the bed frame; the flung-over cupboard; tall chest of drawers shoved to one side. The abandoned attempt at pushing it over. The crash point where the reluctant chest of drawers and wardrobe met... there could be nothing hidden back there. Every furniture angle suggesting the desperate search there must have been. And blocking the outer doorway, the mahogany wardrobe, part-toppled, that Celeste must have clambered over at the sound of Floyd and Jonathan getting near.

And everywhere ripped-apart bundles of clothes.

Wheeler crept back from the chaos, light-headed. Turning, she thought she saw a shadow on the stairs.

"Whey Tant'Celeste gone?" Donelle appeared on the landing as Wheeler made her way back to her room. She swept past him, not answering.

Scooting around her belongings, Wheeler's eyes lighted on her school Keds waiting on the other side of her books. She cut across the room, grabbed her Keds and backed up to the window. Pausing, she gazed at her sisters still asleep on the bed. They lay either side of the mattress with a small space between them.

She sister di' fall on d'ground...

Wheeler watched Adele, remembering. Adele's neck strained away from her pillow.

A knocking below. Innez shouted from the stairs. "Adele! Hesta! All-you get up. Come start getting food ready."

Adele shot up as if pulled. Her eyes landed on Wheeler standing motionless before the window.

"A-*dell*!"

"H-gh? Y-eh... We *coming*!" She shook Hesta. "Y'in hear she calling?"

They flung about grumbling and organising.

Dey could see her?

"You go in d'shower. Ah go make d'cocoa tea."

At a stroke, her sisters had become their daylight selves, Adele leading, Hesta quarrelling as they left.

Innez called out again. "All-you in coming?"

Hesta came back, snatching her bath towel.

Wheeler dropped to the floor. With wide, nervous eyes she watched Hesta leave. Then she scooped on her right Ked. Pounded on the other one. Tied her shoelaces and leapt up off the floor.

As Wheeler strolled by their bedroom door, Jonathan lay on his bed, one hand behind his head. Donelle sat on the floor opposite, bent knees visible.

No need to run. Yet.

Cat-like, Wheeler approached the final bedroom. Prowled alongside the sombre sitting room— RUN!

Out on the veranda, soaring towards the Cut, she became airborne. Flying over the steps, she heard the sounds of the house: Donelle and Jonathan chatting about this and that… about Celeste… waiting to go downstairs. Hesta under the shower. Adele crunching the cocoa stick. Heard the silent chaos in Celeste's bedroom.

Sensing the weight of a mighty hand on her shoulder, arms flailing, gasping free, Wheeler turned round: There was no one there, no one below or behind, just the blameless drop of little steps.

Her legs and arms were shaking but she did not feel any pain. Wheeler thought about her mother. A soft souring in her stomach competed with her trembling legs.

How dey go tell her? How she goan feel?

Approaching the tall iron gate leading to Geraldine and Morgan's house, Wheeler anticipated the noise it would make. Leaving the gate to its swift, heavy clang, she climbed up the steps.

Acknowledgements

Special thanks to my editor, Neil Griffiths, for his support and his kindness, as well as his love of this book from early on. Many thanks to Sarah Terry and James Tookey.

My undying thanks to Weatherglass Books.

—

Thank you, Toby Litt.

THE PAGES OF THE SEA

ANNE HAWK

First published in 2024
by Weatherglass Books

Copyright © 2024 Anne Hawk

All rights reserved. No part of this publication may be reproduced or
transmitted in any form or by any means, electronic or mechanical,
including photocopy, recording or any information storage and retrieval
system, without permission in writing from the publisher.

This book is a work of fiction. Names, characters, businesses,
organizations, places and events are either the product of the author's
imagination or used fictitiously. Any resemblance to actual persons, living
or dead, or events is entirely coincidental.

A CIP record for this book is published by the British Library

ISBN: 978-1-7395707-2-9

Cover design: Luke Bird
Typesetting: James Tookey

Printed in the U.K. by TJ Books, Padstow

www.weatherglassbooks.com

Weatherglass
Books